ROBERTA LEIGH

and then came love

HARLEQUIN BOOKS
toronto-winnipeg

This edition © Roberta Leigh 1974

First published 1954

SBN 373-70568-9
Harlequin Presents edition published November 1974

Printed in Canada.

CHAPTER ONE

MATTHEW Armstrong lounged against the marble mantlepiece and wondered irritably why he had come to Violet Taunton's cocktail party. It was obvious she had only invited him because her husband had told her to do so. His eyes moved over the chattering crowd: women in the latest fashions — most of them ridiculous; men looking either like tailor's dummies in correct lounge suits or like long haired pop singers, and all of them with the same affected voices and unnatural laughter. What did he have in common with them?

As he shifted his weight a hard knob of marble dug into his spine, and he turned round to see the head of a fatuous cherub perpetuated in marble. Damn it all, there wasn't even a chair to sit on! How did the Tauntons expect thirty people to squeeze into this cramped lounge when there was barely space for a dozen? Sipping the mediocre sherry he wondered why Robert Taunton couldn't sell his business over an office desk instead of making a social affair of it. But then these people never liked to call a spade a spade — they dressed everything up as if they were ashamed of money; either of making or losing it.

Idly he swilled the sherry from one side of his glass to the other, then tiring of this, edged his finger round his collar. Lord it was hot. He moved to the window and bent to open it, but it was stuck tight and he looked longingly out at the garden, shrouded in October mist. The atmosphere in the alcove was clearer than by the fireplace, and he turned back to watch the people.

His eyes ranged round the room, pausing as they fell on the figure of a tall girl, moving away and then coming back to rest on her again. He wondered why she had bothered to come, for she made no effort to hide her boredom. Dressed without pretence to fashion, she was the only woman in the room with no jewellery; her silvery fair hair was drawn back with a wide velvet band and her face was almost devoid of makeup. The man at her side was leaning forward to catch her interest, but her expression did not change and Matthew thought no woman had the right to remain so impervious to the attention being paid her.

"There you are, Mr. Armstrong!" It was his hostess. "Would you like another drink?"

"No, thanks."

Violet Taunton racked her brains to find something to say. If Robert had to sell the business, why couldn't he find a more presentable buyer, instead of this crag of a man who obviously couldn't — or wouldn't — mix at a party? But she chattered aimlessly until, with characteristic bluntness, Matthew interrupted her.

"Who's the girl over there? The one with fair hair."

"Stella Percy — Mrs. Edgar Percy's daughter, you know."

"Never heard of Mrs. Edgar Percy," came the blunt reply. "What's she famous for?"

"Her husband — her late husband I mean — was in the Foreign Office."

"Not the sort of man I'd have been likely to meet," Matthew chuckled. "But I'd like to meet the daughter. Will you introduce me?"

"Of course." Relieved that he was taking himself off her hands, Violet Taunton led him across the room. "Stella dear, a most distinguished visitor of ours wants to meet you. He's a friend of Robert's, so do be nice to him."

She flitted away, clutching the neglected young man by his arm, and Matthew laughed. "I'm afraid

6

Mrs. Taunton forgot what she came for and didn't introduce us. I'm Matthew Armstrong." He put out a large hand and caught the girl's in such a strong grasp that she winced. "I'm sorry — did I hurt you?"

"A bit." Her voice was as cool as her smile.

"I've been watching you from over there" — he indicated the alcove — "and you're the only one who had the courage to look as bored as I felt. What made you come?"

Stella's eyes widened at the directness of his question. "Why does one ever come to parties? I could ask you the same."

"Business," he said promptly. "That's the only thing that'd bring me to a do like this."

"What sort of business?" she asked, for want of something to say.

"The business of making money!"

"There you are, Armstrong!" They both turned as Robert Taunton came up. "Hullo, Stella, so you've met our Yorkshire lion? Trust him to pick the prettiest girl in the room."

"I don't know about that," Matthew put in, "but she's the only one I fancy."

Stella coloured, but Robert Taunton's fingers tightened warningly on her arm. "You're frank, Armstrong, that's what I like about you. A business man should always be frank."

"Then what about you being frank enough to have our little talk?" the Yorkshireman demanded.

"Not here, old boy. Come to my office in the morning."

"My train leaves at nine-thirty, so it'll have to be before that or not at all."

"But my dear fellow, you can't go back without settling things!"

"I haven't been the one who's been dallying. You have a business to sell and I came down to buy it. All I got was an invitation to this party."

7

"I didn't think it was so urgent," Taunton said lamely.

"It isn't for me, but I thought it was for *you*."

Stella edged away. "If you want to talk business —"

"We can't talk here," Matthew said quickly, "so there's no need for you to go. I'll expect you at my hotel at eight in the morning, Taunton. If you can't manage it, there's no more to be said."

"I'll be there, Armstrong. On the dot." With a glance at Stella that spoke volumes, Robert Taunton moved away to join another group of people.

"Do you usually conduct your business like that, Mr. Armstrong?" Stella's voice was cold with distaste.

"What did I do wrong?"

"Everything. I don't think anyone's spoken to Robert like that in his life!"

"More's the pity. If someone had he mightn't be selling his business now. Don't look so upset, lass. It won't do him any harm."

"I'm not upset, only amused by your behaviour."

"Well as long as I've amused you, I don't mind." He took a leather case from his pocket, extracted a cigarette and put the case back.

Not until he had done so, did Stella speak. "Do you think I could have a cigarette too? If you can spare one, that is."

His eyes narrowed but in silence he offered her one and lit it with a long, curling flame from a metal lighter.

"Make these myself," he said, snapping it shut and holding it out on his broad palm. "A thousand a day we turn out, and reckon they last a lifetime."

"I thought it was a dying business," she remarked coolly.

"People will always smoke. They'll find a safe cigarette before long. There's too much money at stake for them not to!"

8

"You seem interested in money."

"Aren't you?" she shrugged, and he continued: "There's nothing wrong with money, as long as you come by it honestly."

"But it's such a boring subject."

"Not to me," he grinned. "But I'll talk about something else if you prefer. What about letting me treat you to dinner?"

"I'm glad you aren't inviting me to go dutch," she said dryly.

He reddened. "We talk differently where I come from. I didn't mean —"

"I know," she said quickly. "I was only teasing."

"Then how about it?"

"I'm afraid I can't. I'm — I'm busy."

The smile left his face. "In that case I might as well get the night train back to Leeds. I can't see Taunton keeping an eight o'clock appointment. He doesn't look an early riser to me!"

"But he's promised to come. You can't not be there!"

"I've wasted enough time as it is."

Stella wondered wildly if she could signal Robert that his guest was leaving, but he was nowhere to be seen — not even Violet was visible in the throng of people — and she turned back to the Yorkshireman with a smile that was as appealing as she could make it.

"Will you stay overnight if I have supper with you?"

His heavy face lit up. "That's a temptation I can't resist."

"All right. I'll get my coat and meet you in the hall."

Powdering her nose in Violet's bedroom, Stella reflected that Robert would certainly have to stand her a drink for this. Why in heaven's name had the man taken a fancy to her? From his gusty conversation she would not have considered herself the type to appeal to him.

Picking up her worn fur coat, she went downstairs to find the stocky figure waiting for her. In a heavy top-coat he looked even broader, his hands in their leather gloves larger than ever as he propelled her down the steps to a waiting cab.

"I thought we'd go to the Savoy. Would you like that?"

"Anyone would like it."

"I dare say you go there often?"

She shook her head and he climbed into the taxi beside her. "I'd have thought a girl like you went out a lot. The men in London must be blind!"

"Not blind, Mr. Armstrong. Hard up!"

"Well, there's no shame in poverty. I was hard up myself once, so I know what it's like." She shifted slightly and he peered at her. "Not boring you, am I?"

"No. I moved because I was in a draught."

"You wouldn't feel the cold if you had a bit more fat on your bones."

"I wouldn't get taken to the Savoy either."

He laughed — a loud laugh that boomed in the confined space of the cab. "Rubbish! I like a woman with a bit of fat on her."

"Your taste isn't universal!"

"I'm pretty good at knowing what the public wants. That's made me a success."

"You're talking business again!"

"Sorry." He glanced out. "We've arrived. Once you've got a good meal inside you, you won't feel cold."

In the restaurant, a whispered word with the head waiter brought them to a table by the window some distance from the orchestra.

"I hope you don't mind sitting here," Matthew apologized, "but I hate being played at while I eat."

10

"As a matter of fact I prefer it when I'm not dressed."

For a moment he did not understand her. "Oh, you mean evening dress. Never mind lass, you look fine to me."

He turned his attention to the wine list and Stella studied him as he bent his square face over it, the light glinting on the grey in his hair. The blunt fingers that held the card proclaimed him a man who had worked with his hands, while the heavy gold watch round one powerful wrist bore witness to his success. Looking at the set of his wide mouth and the lines down each side it, she knew she would not like to come up against him in the business he spoke about so freely; yet when he glanced up at her he seemed so kind and unaffected that she could not help warming to him.

"That's better, lass. It's the first time you've smiled since we arrived. You've no idea how it changes your face."

"Does my face need changing?"

"Of course not. It was just my tactless way of talking."

Yet there was an indifference about her that struck him as unnatural, and he was pleased to see it change to animation as she enjoyed the good food set before her.

"Smoking a bit much, aren't you?" he asked as she lit another cigarette. "It's a pity to spoil hands like yours."

She looked at the nicotine stains on her fingers. "They're useless hands anyway."

"You're too young to feel useless. What do you do with yourself?"

"Nothing."

"No wonder you're bored! Don't you work?"

"No. Mother's the type who thinks girls ought to marry, not go out to work."

11

"Did you never want to do anything?"

She regarded her hands. "I wanted to be a pianist, but finances wouldn't run to it."

"I thought folks like you had plenty of money."

She smiled. "Appearances are deceptive. I think most of the money has gone North!"

His laugh boomed out and she glanced round self-consciously, relieved to see that no one appeared to notice.

Suddenly he stood up. "That reminds me of something. Will you excuse me a minute?"

She watched him make his way across the dining-room and wondered why he wore such heavy suiting when he had obviously gone to the trouble of having it well tailored. It made him look heavier than he probably was. She was stubbing out her cigarette when he loomed up beside her and thrust a package into her lap.

"What is it?"

"Open it and see — that's the quickest way to find out."

With embarrassed furtiveness she did as he said and the paper fell back to disclose a huge bottle of scent. Chanel No. Five. Obviously.

Scarlet-faced she re-wrapped it and handed it back. "I can't accept this, Mr. Armstrong."

"Why not? All girls like perfume."

"That's beside the point. But I don't know you — I couldn't accept such a gift."

"Don't be stupid! I bring stacks of this stuff down with me. They make nice presents for manufacturers' wives. Now no more arguing. You're to keep it."

Silently she placed the package beside her handbag. How crude the man was. Offering her a gift in public and then ranting on about his manufacturers' wives. It served her right for accepting his invitation.

With an effort she forced herself to listen to his conversation, and though she made the right responses

12

at the right time, she was glad when he suggested they leave.

"Where do you live?" he asked, helping her into a cab.

"Kensington."

"You look the type to have a country mansion."

"We did have, years ago."

"What happened?"

"Death duties and taxes."

"That was crazy. A good accountant could have —"

"My father never thought about it," she interrupted.

"More's the pity." He leaned towards her. "Do you have any family apart from your mother?"

"My brother Adrian." Resenting his inquisition she made her reply brief, though he did not take the hint.

"What does he do?"

"He's still at school."

"Tell me about him."

"There's nothing to tell. He's eighteen and wants to take up music."

"Anything stopping him?"

She hesitated. "A matter of money."

His reply was cut short by the cab drawing up with a lurch.

"Please don't bother to see me up — stay in the cab and he'll take you back." Hastily she stepped on to the pavement and held out her hand. "Goodnight, Mr. Armstrong."

"May I ring you when I'm in London again?"

She smiled but did not reply, and he watched her mount the steps.

"Goodnight," he called. "I'll be seeing you." Then to the driver: "Back to where we started, lad, and make it snappy. I've an early call in the morning."

He settled back into the corner with a sigh and closed his eyes. Stella. Stella. A star, cold and distant. Yet her very aloofness filled him with desire.

13

Strange that he, a man of forty, should suddenly meet a girl who could attract him so strongly.

The cab swung into the Strand and with a thud something fell against his hand. With an exclamation he picked it up and saw that it was the perfume he had given her. For an instant he felt an upsurge of anger, then gave a chuckle. For all her aloofness she had a mind of her own. It would be a pleasure to get to know her.

CHAPTER TWO

LOOKING back on her evening with Matthew Armstrong, Stella knew she had met a man to whom social convention meant nothing. But after a few days she forgot about him and slipped back into her aimless routine of meeting friends, going to the cinema during the afternoon and occasionally — under protest — visiting a hairdresser.

"Who's to know whether I wash my hair myself or have it set?" she argued with her mother. "It always looks the same in the end — straight and soft."

"Because you don't take pride in yourself. Honestly, Stella, you don't care how you look. You aren't still pining to study music, are you?"

"After all these years!" Stella looked at her hands. "I probably didn't have it in me anyway."

"What's to stop you practising?"

"Practising won't help. It's too late. But I'm not worrying about myself, Mother, it's Adrian. What's going to happen to him? It's bad enough for me, but I may get married; he's got to have a career."

Mrs. Percy's face sharpened with concern. "I want Adrian to be a pianist as much as you do, but we simply can't afford it."

"We could economize more. In dress, for example."

"And save a hundred pounds a year? Even if Adrian got a grant for the Academy, it would cost much more to keep him there. Besides, it would be years before he could fend for himself."

"But he leaves school at the end of this term. He must do *something*."

Mrs. Percy sighed deeply. "If only your father had made some provision for us . . ."

"Didn't you ever talk about money with him?"

"Certainly not. I always assumed we had enough."

"But you were always complaining about being hard up."

"We had to live on a fixed income," came the tight-lipped protest, "but we could always do what we wanted within reason." A pencil-thin eyebrow rose above a pale blue eye. "If only you could make a good marriage. What's happened to Martin Randall?"

Stella laughed. "The chinless wonder of Chelsea! I know you want me off your hands, darling, but you don't want to sacrifice me, do you?"

Mrs. Percy sighed. "If only Charles were in a better position. I can't understand him. Most lawyers can afford to marry once they're in practice."

"He's got a high standard," Stella interposed. "And an invalid mother who's very demanding."

"Then his uncle should help him. If he and his precious son weren't so crazy about sailing they'd have time to think about Charles. After all, until Anne has a son, he's second in line to the title."

"He doesn't think about *that*," Stella smiled. "His uncle and cousin will probably outlive him. Anyway, Anne says she wants a dozen children!"

Mrs. Percy looked pained. "It's not a joking matter. I'm worried about you and Charles. You've known each other for years and neither of you are getting any younger."

"He's only thirty. That's not old."

"Not for a man perhaps, but what about you? You're twenty-five, Stella, and you ought to be married."

"If only I'd had the sense to learn shorthand and typing," Stella ran her hands impatiently through her fine blonde hair. "It's not too late even now."

"You'd hate working in an office."

"I hate being idle!"

"You take care of the flat," her mother protested, "and you do all the cooking and shopping. No housewife does more."

"Not unless she has children," Stella said dryly, and suddenly threw her arms wide. "I'm bored, Mother. Bored to death!"

"Boredom is a state of mind." Mrs. Percy went over to the mirror and patted a dyed brown curl into place. "At least you've got my figure. You'll never have to worry about getting fat." She moved to the door. "By the way, I won't be in for dinner — I'm playing bridge with Betty Sands. What are you doing?"

"Dining with Charles."

"Give him my love. That's all I can afford!"

The door closed behind her and Stella moved across to the mirror. Although her mother had not meant it, the reference to her age had hurt. In another few years Charles might not find her attractive. But that was ridiculous, Charles loved her, and if he had enough money would marry her tomorrow. She sighed and irrationally thought of Matthew Armstrong. How different the two men were: Where one was forthright the other was diplomatic; where Armstrong was determined and matter-of-fact, Charles was vacillating and punctilious. Both men revealed their characters in their speech and mannerisms, Charles's voice correct and well modulated, Armstrong's rough and broad. What a pity Charles did not have Matthew's money, or Matthew Charles's polish!

Promptly at seven o'clock Charles Heyward arrived, and as she led him into the living-room she felt she had enacted this scene many times before.

"Hullo, Stella dear. Pleasant day?"

"The usual. And you?"

"Not too bad."

"There's some sherry in the cabinet," she volunteered. "Help yourself and pour me one."

Meticulously he placed two glasses on the salver on the sideboard, poured out the sherry and handed her one. "Good health."

She had the glass to her lips when the door-bell

17

pealed. "Who on earth can that be? Mother's got her key."

"I'll go." Charles put down his glass and went out.

A moment later he returned, Matthew Armstrong following hard on his heels with the largest bouquet of flowers she had ever seen.

"I'm unexpected, but I hope not unwelcome." He held out the flowers. "Here, you'd better have these, I feel silly with them."

"They're lovely," Stella murmured, avoiding Charles's eyes. "Thank you so much."

Matthew looked from her to Charles. "I hope I'm not intruding?"

"Not at all," she said politely, and introduced them.

Matthew shook Charles's hand heartily. "Any friend of Stella's is a friend of mine!" He turned to her. "I hope you don't mind me calling you Stella? Up in Leeds I couldn't think of you any other way."

"I don't mind, Mr. Armstrong," she said stiffly.

There was an uncomfortable pause, then Charles went to the sideboard. "Would you care for a drink?"

"A whiskey, please."

"There's only sherry, I'm afraid."

"That'll be grand."

Matthew accepted the glass and eyed Heyward speculatively. The man was obviously used to playing host here. Tall and slim, with a sallow complexion and dark, straight hair, he was the sort of person he had expected Stella to know, his appearance as correct as his manner, his polite aloofness identical to hers.

"Are you in London for long?" Charles enquired.

"That depends. I haven't had a holiday for a couple of years, and I can do with a change."

"Why didn't you go to Blackpool?" Stella said lightly. "It's so much nearer."

"And cooler," Matthew smiled. "No one in their

18

senses goes to Blackpool in the winter." He turned to Charles. "Were you and Stella on the way out?"

"As a matter of fact we were, but don't hurry over your sherry."

Matthew drained his glass. "It's my own fault — I should have telephoned to say I was coming."

Stella put her glass on the sideboard. "I'm surprised you managed to get away from your factory."

"Nothing's impossible if you want it enough."

There was a short pause, then Stella went to the door. "I'll get my wrap, Charles. I'm sure you'll forgive us, Mr. Armstrong . . ."

"That's all right. Going to the theatre?"

"No, as a matter of fact —"

"If it's just for dinner what about the two of you being my guests?"

"I'm afraid we can't," she said quickly. "We've already arranged our evening."

She returned with her coat to find him still standing in the middle of the room. When on earth would he take the hint and go?

"Charles dear, we really must leave."

Matthew set his glass on the mantlepiece. "Can I give you a lift? I've a cab outside."

Charles shook his head. "Thanks, but I've got a car."

"In that case I'm overstaying my welcome."

Pointedly Stella said nothing, and Matthew went to the door and opened it. As she came abreast of him he caught her arm. "Aren't you going to put the flowers in water?"

"I haven't time. I'll do it when I get back."

Sitting over an indifferent meal Stella began to feel ashamed of her rudeness, her conscience in no way appeased by Charles's comment on the subject.

"Don't you think you were hard on Armstrong, darling? After all, he came all the way from Leeds to see you."

"I didn't ask him to come. Anyway, he's so thick-skinned he probably didn't notice." Charles's silence made her anger flare. "Anyway, why should you care? Or don't you mind my having another suitor!"

"Of course I mind. But that's got nothing to do with your being polite."

"Next time I'll kiss him hello!" She retorted.

"No you won't." Unexpectedly he leaned over and caught her hand. "If only we could afford to get married." His grip tightened. "Why don't we? Lots of couples marry on far less."

"You never thought so last week," she reminded him. "Or have you suddenly lowered your standards?"

He coloured. "Sometimes one can be too cautious. Maybe that's my trouble. What about it, Stella?"

"What about your mother?" she countered. "I wouldn't want to start our marriage living with another woman."

"We'd have to. I couldn't afford to set her up on her own."

"You could, if she'd lower her standards. *Must* she live in Mayfair?"

"She refuses to move. I've tried to reason with her but it's hopeless. Or maybe I'm not strong enough."

Stella did not refute his remark.

"Perhaps I should have gone into business," he went on. "Like your Yorkshire friend."

"You'd have hated it. You're not competitive enough. Stick to your dusty old documents."

They finished their coffee in silence and drove straight back to the flat. Charles refused to come up for his usual nightcap and bade her such a cool goodnight that she knew he was still hurt by her remark.

Darn Matthew, she thought crossly, he had no business to come without warning. It had made her rude to him and quarrel with Charles. She walked into the drawing-room and stared resentfully at the bouquet still lying on the piano. The man must have bought the florist's shop! Impatiently she picked up the flowers and carried them into the kitchen, dumping them unceremoniously into a sink full of water. What a waste of money!

Against her will she smiled. How ridiculous he had looked behind the huge bunch of flowers — like an old-fashioned suitor calling on his lady-love!

But the following morning the incident did not seem quite as amusing. The poor man had meant well: if she was contemptuous because he was uncouth and self-made he had every right to despise her for being a useless parasite. There was some excuse for his bad manners, none for hers, and on an impulse she dialled the Savoy.

On the line his voice was brusque and businesslike. "Armstrong here."

"It's Stella Percy," she said quickly. "I'm ringing up to apologize for last night. I'm afraid I was rather rude."

"Rude?"

"Yes." Bother the man. Couldn't he make it easier for her? "I'm sorry I had to rush off when you'd only just arrived."

"Never mind, it was my own fault for expecting you to be free at such short notice. Next time I'll write."

She could think of nothing to say and there was an awkward pause.

"Are you still there?" he asked.

"Yes, but if you're busy I'll —"

"No, don't go. I want to talk to you. I'd an idea you were angry at my turning up the way I did. I don't suppose you're free tonight, are you? I'm not going back to Leeds till the end of the week and I'd like to see you again."

She floundered, unable to think of an excuse. "Well, I — actually, as a matter of fact, I am free."

"That's great! We can go to a show. Is there anything you'd like to see?"

"I'll leave it to you."

"Right. I'll call for you at six-thirty."

The receiver went dead in her hand. Well, that was that. He had accepted her apology with an ease which had made it seem superfluous, and she was unaccountably piqued.

Mrs. Percy made no comment when Stella told her she was going out with a man she had met at the Tauntons' cocktail party, but her surprise was patent when she opened the door to Matthew that evening.

"Hullo, Mrs. Percy, I'd have known you were Stella's mother anywhere! You're an older edition of your daughter."

"Oh! I'm afraid I didn't get your name."

"Matthew Armstrong." He followed her into the drawing-room.

"Do sit down, Mr. Armstrong, Stella won't be long."

"I hope not. The curtain goes up at seven-thirty and I don't want to miss the beginning. Some of these modern plays are hard enough to understand as it is without coming slap in the middle!"

"I suppose so. But then young women are rarely punctual."

"Most of the girls I know are. They can't afford not to be. If they don't clock in at eight, out they go."

"You can hardly be expected to clock in at a theatre."

"More's the pity." He stood up as Stella came into the room, his eyes warm as they travelled over her. "You look wonderful, lass! You should always wear red. It gives you a bit of colour." He caught her arm. "I was just telling your mother that I like my women to be punctual."

"It's a commendable trait," she said, and avoiding her mother's eyes, hurriedly led him out.

The play Matthew had chosen was a serious drama and she was surprised at the intelligence of his criticism. In evening dress he looked almost distinguished, his tanned face and powerful shoulders exuding a masculine strength that far exceeded Charles's. But he had none of the younger man's polish, and though polite, it was with a take-it-or-leave-it air that held none of the deference to which she was accustomed.

Later, dancing at a restaurant, she was equally surprised at his competence on the floor, for though her high heels made her slightly the taller, he was so broad that she was not conscious of her height. Returning to the table, she was amused when he ordered a second portion of vegetables, and somewhat taken aback when he remarked on her own small appetite.

"You had a better meal the other night at the Savoy. Are you ill?"

"I'm not hungry."

"What did you do with yourself all day?"

"I did some shopping and then had tea with a girl friend." She shrugged. "I'm sure it wasn't as exciting as your day."

"You can say that again! I'm not surprised you're fed up with the life you lead. You should get married and have children. You'd have no time to get bored then!"

"I'm not particularly maternal."

"No woman is till she's had 'em!"

She smiled. "Men always seem to think they know what's best for us."

"I don't profess to know what's good for women in general, but I do think I know what'd be best for you."

She averted her eyes from his intent gaze. "This is rather a nice band, isn't it? Do they have places like this in Leeds?"

"No. There's always the hotels and the golf club, of course, but one gets tired of seeing the same faces."

"Why do you stay there, then?"

"I was born and bred in Yorkshire and I shall die there."

"If everyone said that, what would happen to the pioneer spirit?"

"It doesn't take much pioneer spirit to move to London, but I'll not argue with you."

"I thought you'd love an argument," she smiled. "You strike me as being —" she floundered, and he finished the sentence for her.

"Obstinate eh? I suppose I am. Still it's made me a millionaire, so I'm not complaining. If I'd been soft I'd still be earning two pounds a week. To get to the top, you've got to fight."

"Not everyone knows what to fight *for.*"

"Everyone has *something* they want," he insisted. "I know I have."

"I'd have thought you already had everything you wanted."

Matthew studied her pale triangular face and the fall of soft blonde hair that swung against her cheekbones. "I still need one thing," he said softly.

"I suppose you mean a wife?"

"Yes." Ruefully he ran a hand over his hair. "Or do I strike you as too old?"

"Of course not." She pushed back her chair. "Can we dance again?"

He led her on to the floor and with a sense of relief she gave her mind to the music.

Matthew guided her firmly, wishing he had the courage to tell her what was in his mind. Her reception of him last night had been disconcerting, to say the least, and if he had not appreciated the effort it must have cost her to telephone and apologize he would not have seen her again.

During his weeks up North he had wondered if she was as attractive as he had imagined, or if he had been particularly susceptible at the Tauntons' boring party? He had known far lovelier girls than this one — why should she hold his interest more than any of the others? Yet his desire to see her again had compelled him to come back when common sense had told him it might end in disaster, and his delight in meeting her again had confirmed his fears: he was in love with her.

"Are you free tomorrow night?" he asked abruptly. "I only came down to see *you*."

"That makes it very difficult for me to say I'm busy."

"I want to make it difficult. *Will* you see me?"

"Yes, but —"

"No buts. It's all settled."

CHAPTER THREE

FOR THE rest of that week and the beginning of the next Matthew remained in London, bluffly overriding Stella's objection at seeing him too frequently. To begin with Mrs. Percy regarded him as a joke, but as the days went by she grew concerned.

"Don't you think you're seeing too much of Mr. Armstrong, Stella?"

"Don't worry, Mother, he's going back to Leeds in a few days."

They were in Stella's bedroom, a narrow box of a room which, in better days, had served as one of the servants' sitting-rooms. But Stella liked it because it overlooked a belt of trees, and when the wind blew the rustle of the leaves coming through the high window made a melancholy accompaniment to her thoughts.

"Even so, why give a man like that any encouragement?" Her mother persisted. "He's just the kind to get ideas from a few casual evenings."

"He isn't a schoolboy."

"And he isn't the sort of man to indulge in platonic friendship either! You've gone out with him every night this week."

"I don't know why you're making such a fuss! You've never worried about whom I've gone out with before."

"Because I've never known you to go out six nights in succession with the same man. And he's not even your type!"

"He's different and amusing."

"He's certainly different," Mrs. Percy sniffed.

"Don't look so worried, Mother. I'm not planning on marrying him."

"I should hope not! He's the last man I'd want as

a son-in-law. Anyway, what about Charles? You've always spoken as if you'd marry *him* if you had the chance."

"I suppose I would," Stella said moodily. "Though sometimes I think he'd bore me to death! At least Matthew makes me laugh."

"It's ridiculous to compare Charles with *him*. I grant you Mr. Armstrong may be more masculine, but he's such a boor." Mrs. Percy went to the door. "Don't forget that men like Charles are reserved. This man's kisses may be more exciting, but —"

"Matthew's never kissed me," Stella interrupted.

"Oh." Her mother was momentarily floored. "Well, that's something to be thankful for. At least when you're with Charles I know you're safe!"

The door closed behind her and Stella smiled. Safe! That was the trouble. She was always so safe with him she might as well go out with her brother! She was still young enough to want a good time, to want excitement and the thrill of the chase, and with Charles she had neither.

If Matthew kissed her he would not bother to be restrained, and sometimes coming home with him in the taxi she wondered if he was going to take her in his arms. But he never attempted to touch her except when they were dancing, and she was half ashamed of a secret desire that he should do so.

Although her mother had expressed surprise that she should find it amusing to go out with Matthew, Stella genuinely enjoyed her evenings with him for he had a sense of humour and a quick mind. He told her of his years in the tool factory near Armley where he was born, and though he made light of his years of work, she guessed they had been hard and admired his strength in forging such a successful career for himself.

She stood up and went to the wardrobe, but her

sparse collection of dresses afforded little choice. It would have to be the black one again.

That night he took her to dinner at a club in Knightsbridge and over the meal plied her with questions about her family. It was the first time he had done so since the evening they had met, and this time she answered more willingly.

"It's a trite story," she explained. "At least as long as you're not involved personally — the way I am."

"Your father died poor, you mean," Matthew said in his usual outspoken manner.

She nodded. "I was just seven and Adrian was four. Mother had to bring us both up on her pension and it wasn't easy."

"A Foreign Office pension is a sight more than most folk get!"

"It depends how one wants to live," Stella retorted.

"I take it your mother found living hard?"

"Extremely. I wanted to study music but we couldn't afford it, and now Adrian's in the same position."

Matthew sipped his brandy. "Wouldn't he get a student grant?"

"It isn't only the fees. It's the extras. And we simply haven't got the money."

"So what will he do?"

"Get a job. He's bitter about it, and I can't say I blame him. It wasn't until last term that he found out how hard up we were. Mother always insisted he shouldn't know the truth."

"Then she was a fool," Matthew said with his usual bluntness.

"She was foolish," Stella corrected. "There's a difference." She shook her head. "I only hope Adrian faces facts. He's intelligent but spoilt."

"No son of mine would be spoilt at eighteen!" came the retort.

"That's an easy thing to say. But not so easy to carry out."

"You're fond of your brother, aren't you?"

She nodded. "We were together a lot. My parents were abroad for many years and Adrian and I lived with a cousin. She was quite nice with me, but she didn't seem to like little boys. Poor Adrian had a tough time."

Matthew's face softened. "You've never spoken with such love in your voice. I like to hear it."

"I'm not made of stone, you know."

"I didn't mean that." He drained his glass. "It's late. We must be going."

Sitting next to him in the taxi she was more aware of his proximity than ever, his bulk looking so large that she gave an involuntary shiver.

"Cold?"

"A little," she lied.

"I'll close the window." He did so, and as he settled back, put an arm around her shoulders. "You're too thin, lass."

Stella knew he wanted to kiss her, and though filled with uneasiness at the thought, she could not restrain a willing acquiescence as he drew her against him.

"I've wanted to hold you like this for such a long time!"

He placed his lips gently on hers, but fired by the touch of her mouth the pressure increased and his kiss deepened. For a moment she resisted, then with a sigh relaxed against him, feeling that in this big, tender embrace she could find the security and strength she was seeking.

Slowly he drew away and rubbed his cheek against hers, the skin hard and rough. "I didn't know you could kiss like that."

She laughed awkwardly. "Neither did I."

"Seems like we've wasted a lot of time. It's nearly seven weeks since we met."

"You've been up North for most of them."

"I've seen you twelve times," he insisted.

"Do you keep a diary?"

"I don't have to where you're concerned. I remember." He leaned towards her. "I'm going back in the morning."

She was surprised. "That's sudden, isn't it? I thought you were staying until the end of the week."

"I meant to, but there's trouble in one of the factories, and I must deal with it. But I'll be down again as quickly as I can. Will you miss me?"

"Of course." Her eyes twinkled. "And I'll miss your funny accent!"

"Yours sounds just as funny to me."

"I suppose it must. We're not alike even in the way we speak."

Her innocent remark seemed to sober him, and he regarded her intently through the gloom of the cab. "I daresay not, on the surface. I'm hoping we are underneath."

She moved uneasily. "How portentous that sounds!"

"It was meant to. If we — darn it, we're at your flat already. The cab was quicker than I thought. Do you mind if I come in for a while?"

"It's very late," she temporised.

"Alright." He helped her out and kept the door open. "But you won't always be able to get rid of me. I'll be seeing you, Stella. Don't forget me."

"I won't," she promised, and moved hurriedly to the steps, watching from a safe distance as he climbed into the taxi and was driven away.

To her surprise a light was still burning in the drawing-room, and she went in to find her mother sitting in front of the fire. "I thought you'd have been in bed ages ago."

"I want to talk to you, Stella."

"If it's about Matthew —"

"It's more important than that — it's Adrian. He's home."

"But term doesn't end for another month!"

"He's got it into his head that it's useless to stay on. As he can't go to the Academy he says he wants to get a job without wasting any more time."

"Surely he could have waited another few weeks and left decently!"

"He says he can get a job over Christmas if he starts looking for one now."

"Delivering Christmas cards, I suppose? He's pulling your leg."

"No, he isn't. Really, Stella, I wonder whether you understand your brother as well as you say you do! You know all he cares about is music, yet you make a remark like that. This Matthew person isn't having a good influence on you."

"I don't see what Matthew's got to do with it. Anyway, he's going back to Leeds tomorrow."

"At least that's one worry out of the way! For a while I thought you were serious about him."

"Would you mind?"

"Would I *mind?* I'd rather have no son-in-law than one like him!"

"He's very wealthy," Stella said indifferently. "If I married him it might solve a lot of problems, including Adrian."

Her mother stared at her in consternation. "I know we'd both do a lot for Adrian, but I won't have you selling yourself to the highest bidder!"

Stella burst out laughing. "You make me sound like a prize at an auction! Don't forget no one else has put in a bid for me, with the exception of Charles."

"You could do worse than take him."

"I don't love him. Going out with Matthew has at least made me realise that."

31

"You surely don't love this Matthew creature?" her mother said sarcastically.

"I don't know."

"You don't *know?*" Mrs. Percy was aghast. "How far has this gone?"

"He hasn't asked me to marry him, if that's what you mean."

"I should hope not!" Mrs. Percy walked agitatedly round the room. "He's so uncouth I don't know how you can bear him. He might be presentable to look at, but the minute he opens his mouth . . . Really, Stella, people would think you were desperate if you married a man like that!"

"You're such a snob," Stella said mildly. "He's very attractive once you get to know him."

"I knew it," Mrs. Percy shrieked. "It's sex appeal! That's the only way a man like that could attract a girl like you."

"What's wrong with using sex appeal?"

Her mother sniffed. "Charles wouldn't."

"He hasn't got any to use!"

"He's a gentleman. Which is something this — this factory manager could never be!"

Holding on to her temper, Stella walked to the door. "You're adept at destroying illusions, Mother."

"Illusions are better destroyed. Only the very rich or the very poor can afford them."

Getting ready for bed, Stella pondered over her mother's tirade against Matthew. Although he could not help his brusque manner and lack of social graces, it was true they were totally unsuited to each other. One might be swept away by a few kisses, but marriage was a different matter, and lying wakeful in bed she experienced a complete revulsion against him. They had nothing in common, no basis on which to meet except desire, and she was glad he was going back to Leeds in the morning. By the time he returned she would be able to refuse his invitations with impunity.

The moment Stella went in to breakfast the following morning she knew by the sudden silence that Adrian and her mother had been talking about her.

"Hullo, darling, lovely to see you." She kissed her brother, then sat down and took a piece of toast.

"Still as skinny as ever!" Adrian grinned.

"So are you. What made you leave school ahead of time?"

He was studiedly off-hand. "Term's over bar the shouting, and I couldn't see the point of wasting time. If I've got to go into an office I might as well start as soon as possible — unless you can find a rich man to get us out of this hole!"

"Adrian, be quiet and finish your breakfast!" Mrs. Percy said sharply.

"Sorry, Ma," he winked, and bent over his plate.

Stella's eyes rested on him speculatively. From Adrian's point of view it would be easy for her to marry a wealthy man and help them; young boys were so egotistical they did not care how they got what they wanted. Yet looking at him, she felt a stab of compassion that he should be deprived of the chance of using his talent.

With his incessant pounding at the piano and his untidiness and noise, Adrian brought the flat to life, and Stella felt younger and less troubled. That he was curious about Matthew she was well aware, for she caught him pumping Charles one evening when she went into the living-room and as they drove off in his car he mentioned it.

"Adrian seems very interested in Armstrong. Has he reason to be?"

"I haven't seen him for weeks. Certainly not."

"A fortnight," he corrected.

"Have you been keeping count?"

He changed gears. "It's a fortnight since you last stood me up."

"But I explained that was because Matthew had come down expressly to see me —"

"I don't see why he should have done that — unless you encouraged him."

"Aren't you being childish?" Stella said quietly. "After all, he's quite unimportant."

"If I was sure of that I wouldn't argue. But Adrian thinks —"

"Adrian's got no right to think anything! I've never even discussed Matthew with him."

"Even so, he knows you pretty well."

"Not well enough to read my mind! Honestly Charles, you should have more sense than to listen to a school boy."

Charles slowed down. "I'm sorry, my dear. If you tell me there's nothing to worry about, I'll take your word." He lifted her hand on to his knee. "Let's enjoy our evening and no more bickering, eh?"

Stella smiled at him, but inwardly she was fuming with anger. How dare Adrian discuss her affairs with Charles? It might end *his* problems if she became Matthew's wife but it would undoubtedly begin hers! And no matter how much she cared about her brother's future, she had no intention of sacrificing her life to help him achieve his musical ambition. And that was what marriage to Matthew would be: a sacrifice.

CHAPTER FOUR

MATTHEW Armstrong relaxed in the corner of the first-class carriage and let out a gusty sigh. He was on his way to London and Stella. It was nearly a month since he had seen her, a month of continual effort to avert a strike. For the moment things were calm, and if he could settle the position between himself and Stella he would be able to go ahead with a clear mind.

Arriving in London he went straight to his hotel, bathed and changed and then took a taxi to her home. Only when he was half-way there did he remember he had not telephoned first, then characteristically shrugged the thought away. At five o'clock in the evening of a bitterly cold day it was unlikely she would be anywhere except home, and he smiled as he imagined her surprise when he walked in.

He felt like an excited schoolboy when he rang the bell of the shabby front door, his hands moist as footsteps crossed the hall and the door opened to reveal a slim lad with Stella's straight fair hair and brown eyes.

"I bet you're Adrian!" Matthew extended his hand. "You look like your sister. My name's Armstrong."

Adrian smiled charmingly. "Not *the* Mr. Armstrong?"

"Is there more than one?"

"Not as far as my sister's concerned. Do come in."

Matthew walked into the hall, and Adrian threw open the living-room door and announced in stentorian tones: "Mr. Matthew Armstrong!"

There was a gasp of surprise, but Matthew walked straight over to Stella, looking as if he was about to catch her in a bear-like hug.

She side-stepped quickly. "Mother, you remember Matthew?"

Mrs. Percy smiled with difficulty. "I thought you were in Yorkshire?"

"I'm here now!"

"You're lucky you can leave your business so often."

"I've business here, too." He turned to Stella. "I'd like to talk to you alone."

Mrs. Percy stood up. "If I'm in the way —"

"I didn't mean that," he said hastily. "It was just may way of asking Stella to come out with me."

With a tight smile Mrs. Percy sat down again, and Matthew looked at Stella so appealingly that she stood up.

"I'll get my coat."

Relief flooded his face. "That'll be grand!"

Freshening her make-up, Stella wondered irritably why Matthew had to put his foot in it the minute he arrived. Surely he had enough sense to telephone before coming, instead of repeating his last faux pas and blundering in without warning? She went back to the living-room to find him still sitting uncomfortably in the upright chair, his coat over his knees, the thick belt trailing on the floor.

"Let me take your coat and we'll have a drink before we go," she said abruptly.

"I've already offered Mr. Armstrong a drink," her mother put in, "but he doesn't like sherry."

Adrian breached the awkward pause that followed. "Do you live in Leeds itself, Mr. Armstrong?"

"A little bit outside, lad. On the Harrogate Road."

"I suppose you're what they call an industrial magnate?"

Matthew grinned. "Yes. But I'd rather be a personal one!"

No one had any reply to make to this and Adrian

offered him a cigarette. "How many factories do you have?" he asked blandly.

"Six." Matthew held out his lighter. "These are made in one of them."

"How dull!"

"The man who gets his wage packet doesn't think so."

"I'd hate it myself. Music's all I care about."

"Some people would find piano-playing dull."

"There's not much likelihood I will," Adrian said ruefully. "I might even come to you for a job."

"I might even give you one!"

Adrian looked at his mother. "Hear that, Ma? Who said I'd never get a job?"

"Come along, Matthew," Stella broke in. "Let's go."

They left the flat in silence, Stella well aware that the moment the door closed, Adrian and her mother would settle down to a critical discussion of her escort. They stepped out on to the pavement and a cold wind blew against them.

"I'm afraid I didn't ask the cab to wait," Matthew apologized. "I reckoned on having a chat at your place. Never mind, though, I'll find another one."

This was easier said than done and they had to walk the length of Knightsbridge before they managed to flag one down. Stella climbed in quickly and sat shivering in the corner.

"I'm sorry you're cold, lass."

"Why didn't you keep your cab? A ticking meter's never worried you before." She checked herself. "I'm sorry, that was beastly of me."

Instantly he smiled. "You're annoyed with me because I didn't telephone. But I was so anxious to see you . . ." He caught her hand. "I hoped you'd be pleased to see me?"

"Of course I'm pleased."

"Are you really?" He leant eagerly towards her

and she edged away, relieved as the taxi-driver pushed back the communicating window and asked where they wanted to go.

"Better make it the Savoy."

"Again?" Stella said acidly.

"Well, I'm staying there, but if you'd rather go somewhere else, just name the place."

"It's usual for one's escort to arrange the evening."

He looked at her uncertainly, then his face hardened and he turned back to the cabby. "The Savoy," he repeated.

Not having booked a table, they were placed near the door directly in the path of the hurrying waiters, and neither the food nor the wine could quell Stella's irritation.

Arriving at the theatre after dinner she was even more annoyed to find their seats were behind a pillar, and craning her neck to see the stage made her head ache so badly that she was glad when the performance was over.

"Would you like to go somewhere for coffee?" Matthew asked solicitously as they made their way into the foyer.

"It's late. We'd better go home."

"We've been later than this before."

"I know, but I'm tired."

He was immediately concerned. "You should have said so, lass, and we wouldn't have stayed through the show. It was awful anyway."

She moved impatiently ahead of him and waited with chattering teeth while he tried to procure a taxi, watching him lumber up the street only to have it taken by someone else. At last he managed to get one and shouted to her to follow him.

"Come on, lass, it's warmer inside than out!"

She trailed up the street, biting her lip with mortification at the amused glances of several passers-by.

"Was there any need to make such a noise?" she

snapped as she came abreast of him. "I could see you'd got a cab, you didn't have to shout."

"I didn't shout, I only called." He climbed in. "Do you still want to go home?"

"Yes."

They drove back to Knightsbridge in silence, Stella longing for the evening to be over and to be rid of this man. She had had enough. It was time she told him not to bother her any more.

Out of the darkness a big hand closed over hers. "Don't be cross, sweetheart. I know everything's gone wrong this evening."

She was touched in spite of herself. "That's all right. It wasn't your fault. I'm just in a bad mood."

"I'm afraid I put you in it."

She did not contradict him and he lapsed into silence until they drew up at the flat. "Will you have lunch with me tomorrow?"

"I'm busy," she lied.

"Please, Stella. Don't refuse me."

Her resolution to be rid of him weakened. "Very well. Where shall I meet you?"

There was a ghost of a smile on his face. "We'd better say the Dorchester this time!"

She held out her hand. "Goodnight. See you to-morrow."

Alone in the darkness of the cab, Matthew took a small black box from his pocket. He snapped it open and morosely stared at the large diamond. Then with an exclamation of anger he closed the lid and put it away.

When Stella went into the kitchen for breakfast next morning Adrian greeted her with a bow.

"Good-morning, lass. Matthew Armstrong is a grand lad. Right grand!"

"That's not very funny," she said icily.

"I was only trying to bring back romantic memories for you!" He grinned. "Matter of fact, he's not all that bad. And he has what counts, hasn't he? Lovely lolly."

Stella poured herself some coffee. "Has it struck you that I might *like* him?"

"No."

"That's enough, Adrian," Mrs. Percy intervened, and looked at her daughter. "I'm having lunch with Joan Crawley. Will you come with me?"

"I've got a date."

"With a grand lad who shall be nameless?" Adrian asked, and laughingly escaped from the room before Stella could grab him.

Mrs. Percy waited until he was out of earshot. "I thought you weren't going out with that unsufferable man any more."

"I won't be seeing him after today, so you needn't worry."

"That's something to be thankful for. I mean it for your good, Stella, not for mine."

But sitting beside Matthew at lunch Stella realized just how difficult it would be to tell him she didn't intend seeing him again. He seemed in an especially festive mood and was wearing a light grey suit that made him look younger and more attractive. Illogically she thought he was much better-looking than she remembered. Away from him she only recalled the things she disliked; with him she could see his good points — his fine, leonine head with its crest of dark, greying hair, the kindly blue eyes that held so much candour and the firm, wide mouth and determined chin.

He put down the menu and caught her gaze. "I couldn't sleep all last night for thinking of you."

"What a waste of time," she said lightly.

"I'd rather be the judge of that. You're very lovable."

"I'm not in the least lovable. Don't endow me with qualities I haven't got." She looked at her plate. "The food's getting cold."

"I can take a hint! But there's something I want to say and you can't put me off indefinitely!"

The meal over, they sauntered into Hyde Park and he tucked her arm in his. A pale wintry sun shone out of a watery sky and the bare trees offered no protection from the wind. Matthew increased their pace, and as they walked Stella's cheeks began to glow and he felt a throb of satisfaction to have her by his side in the open air instead of in the over-heated atmosphere of a restaurant. She should get into the country more often and have plain whole-some food to put some fat on her bones. His Stella was too brittle-looking, too fine-strung and fragile. He put out a hand to touch a wisp of hair that was blow-ing against her cheek and she looked at him quickly, the colour in her face deepening at the ardour in his gaze.

"Let's sit down now we're warmer." He guided her along a side path to a bench and settled himself with deliberation. "You know I've been coming to London to see you, and I'm going to put my cards on the table. I've not led the life of a saint — I'm a man and I needn't say more — but there comes a time when you want one particular woman to be your wife and the mother of your children, and I want you. I love you, Stella, and I want to marry you."

Stella wished the ground would open and swallow her. Why, oh why hadn't she listened to her mother and stopped seeing him long ago? To refuse him now was so much more cruel than if she had never allowed him to fall in love with her in the first place. Yet he had no right to read so much into a few brief meetings.

"Well sweetheart?" He went to take her in his arms but she moved away.

"No, Matthew, don't! I — I'm sorry you've said what you have. I like you and I enjoy being with you — but I can't marry you."

"If you're thinking of last night —"

"It has nothing to do with last night. It's just that I don't love you."

"Are you in love with someone else. Is it Charles?"

"He can't afford to marry," she prevaricated.

"Do you love him?" he repeated.

She hesitated. To say a firm yes would stop Matthew from repeating his proposal. Yet he had been too honest with her, for her to lie to him. "I like him very much," she admitted. "Our families have been friends for years, but there's never been anything violent in our feelings for each other."

"I couldn't have known you for long without it being violent," Matthew said dryly.

She flushed. "I didn't think you were so susceptible."

"I'm not. Except where you're concerned." He caught her by the shoulders. "Oh Stella, don't you know how beautiful you are? With your dark eyes and your soft hair and that cold mouth that isn't a bit cold when you kiss it."

"Matthew don't! You're imagining things about me."

"I'm not. I know you better than you know yourself. Don't turn me down, lass. We could have a great life together. I'd help your brother and do everything to make you happy. I love you, Stella, I won't take no for an answer."

"You must!" She pulled out of his grasp and stood up. "I can't marry you. I don't love you."

"You haven't given yourself a chance. You're afraid of me."

With a suddenness that took her by surprise he rose and drew her close again, his mouth covering hers before she had a chance to protest. But even in passion he was gentle, his lips soft and tender, caressing her in soft movements that allayed all her fears.

"You see?" he said huskily, drawing slowly away. "If you could stop being afraid of me . . . if you could let yourself go . . ." He took her arm and drew it through his. "I'm going to ask you once more, Stella. Not now, don't look so frightened, but in a little while. Until I do . . . think about it!"

CHAPTER FIVE

Stella found it surprisingly difficult to forget Matthew. She saw Charles frequently during the next few weeks and found him so dull by comparison that she wondered whether he was incapable of passion or was merely subduing it because it was the conventional thing to do.

Christmas came and went and Stella was chagrined that there was no word from Matthew, not even a card. Although she had refused to marry him, it was mortifying that he had not come down to ask her again, nor cared sufficiently to remember her at Christmas. So much for his protestations of love!

January drew to a close and Charles found Adrian a job in the city. At first Mrs. Percy was afraid he might leave it, but he gradually settled down, and after a few weeks informed them he had been given a raise. Indeed, he became so lavish with money, that Stella remonstrated with him.

"I don't want you buying me such things," she said, staring hopelessly at a flimsy negligee, his latest and most exotic gift. "You should save your money, not waste it on me."

"There's plenty more where this comes from," he said airily. "And I like buying you things. You and Ma haven't had it easy, and if I can make it up to you, I will."

"We'd be happier if you saved it," she persisted. "If you had some capital behind you, you could study music if you still wanted to."

"Forget that one," he said sharply. "I'm a working boy now. On the first rung of the ladder and all set to climb."

"Not too quickly," she said before she could stop herself, "or you might fall!"

44

"I'll always have you to pick me up!" He ruffled her hair. "Stop fussing, Stel. I'm not a baby."

But Stella's unease did not abate. If anything it grew worse. Adrian had changed a lot during the last few months. His ties were too loud, his hair too long, and his occasional lapses into the vernacular more and more lurid — an indication of the people with whom he was associating.

Her fears were justified when she came home one night and found him sprawled on the downstairs step, too drunk to move.

She half pulled, half dragged him into the kitchen. "Where have you been to get in this state?" she demanded.

He grinned vacuously. "Out."

"Where?"

"Thash my business. Going to bed. I'm tired." He stood up, then sat down abruptly with a look of comical surprise. "I shay, can't walk."

"I don't wonder. You're drunk."

He giggled and put his head down on the kitchen table. Stella stared at him helplessly. The only remedy she knew was strong black coffee, and she went to the stove and made him some, rousing him to drink it.

An hour later he was looking at her sheepishly over an empty pot.

"Now then," she said sharply, "tell me where you've been and with whom."

"To the Golden Lamp with some friends."

"What were you doing?"

His eyes lowered, hidden by his lids. "Nothing much. One or two deals."

"What sort of deals?"

"Cars — radios — you know the sort of thing. I sell 'em."

"Where do you get them from?"

"Friends. They let me have them at a special price and I sell them around. It's money for jam."

She moistened lips that were dry with fear. "And where do your friends get these cars and radios — from other peoples garages?"

"You're out of your mind! They're not stolen."

"Are you sure?"

"Course I am. They're factory rejects!"

"You mean they're stolen from the factories!"

Adrian jumped up. "I've had enough. I'm going to bed."

"Not till I've finished." Stella was in front of him, barring his way. "You can go to prison for dealing in stolen goods. What's the matter with you, Adrian? You've got a good job and —"

"A good job! Do you call slogging in an office a good job?"

"Not all your friends were rich. What about the ones who've gone to university? I bet most of *them* are living on grants."

"There's a difference between a hard-up student and a hard-up clerk!"

"The only difference is in *your* mind."

"Come off it: At least if you're a student you have a future. But what's *my* future going to be?" He checked himself. "I'm sorry, Stel, I know things haven't been easy for you either. We both wanted the same thing and I've no more right to grumble than you have."

"If only I could help you," she said. "Even if I got a job, by the time we've paid someone to look after the flat, there'd be nothing much left over."

"Ma could do it," Adrian said in sarcastic tones. "I'm sure she'd love to."

"Mother was brought up to a different way of life." Stella resolutely refused to concur with her brother. "She's too old to change now. But you're not! Face facts and make the best of them."

"That's exactly what I am doing! I'm not cut out to be a clerk, and if I can't get to the top I'd rather —"

"End up in prison!" There was an ugly silence. "I'm sorry," Stella said at last, "but I'm trying to make you see sense."

"There's no sense in anything," Adrian's voice was unsteady. "The wrong people have money." He opened the door. "Goodnight Sis."

Lying wakeful in bed, Stella faced the ugly truth. Adrian was a weakling. Unable to pursue his real ambition, he would look for an easy way to make money, regardless of where it led him. Yet what right did she have to condemn him when she was equally as weak? If she had been more determined she could have made a career for herself instead of wistfully waiting for a better tomorrow. As if a better tomorrow ever came! No, if one wanted something, one had to fight for it. It was the only way.

But Adrian would not fight. His behaviour had shown that all too clearly, and a shady deal and a few shady friends would soon develop into something worse. If only he had more spirit, a little of what Matthew called guts.

Even as she asked herself what she could do, the answer stared her in the face. With a brother-in-law like Matthew, Adrian would have the financial ballast he needed. But how could she marry a man she did not love?

She switched on the light and sat up. If it had not been for her mother her feelings for Matthew might have developed. Yet it had been easier for her to send him away than face a barrage of criticism every time she saw him. She remembered the last time they had met: even now the thought made her shiver. Yes, she desired Matthew, but because he had a different outlook and background she despised herself for wanting him instead of Charles.

The thought of Charles brought her to a mental halt. Her marriage to another man would be a terrible blow to his pride. But would anything except his pride be hurt? Charles looked on marriage as an eventuality to be considered with caution. Matthew wanted her tempestuously and needed her to make him happy. If she married him, perhaps love would come later.

Impulsively she went to the writing desk in the corner of her room. Every day counted with Adrian, and if she was going to marry Matthew it would have to be soon. Picking up a pen, she began to write.

"It's a long time since I've heard from you and I hope you are well. It's cold here at the moment and you are wise to stay at home, as there's nothing worse than the impersonality of a hotel in winter. I shall always be pleased to see you when you come to London, and perhaps you will let me know when you do.

> Yours,
>
> Stella"

Was she saying too much or not enough — would he read between the lines or merely think she was writing for politeness' sake? But she could not bring herself to be more explicit. If he had any perception he would know what she was trying to say.

To her chagrin, her letter to Matthew did not bring the immediate reply she had expected, and as the days turned into a week she decided he no longer wanted her. So much for her self-sacrifice!

There was little to occupy her apart from running the flat, and though she indulged in an orgy of cleaning, by early afternoon of each day her chores were done and she would practice her music and brood on the opportunities lost to her and Adrian through lack of money and — even more galling — lack of perseverance.

One Sunday afternoon nearly a fortnight later, she sat at the piano, the curtains drawn against the quick descent of night. The standard lamp was lit, shedding a pool of light above the music as her fingers moved over the keys, the calm flow of a Brahms sonata lulling her into placidity until she struck the last note.

"It's the first time I've heard you play, lass."

She swung round to see Matthew in the centre of the room. "I didn't hear you arrive!"

"Adrian let me in." He drew off his gloves and stuffed them into his coat pocket. "I'll put this in the hall."

When he came back she was standing in front of the fire. "Have you had tea?"

"Never ask a Yorkshireman that. I'd love a cup!"

"I'll make you some. Sit down and get warm."

She was buttering the toast when she felt someone watching her and turned to see him in the kitchen doorway.

"Can I help?"

"No, thanks." She spoke quickly and nervously. "It's all finished except for the tea."

"Shall I warm the pot?"

"I'll do it. Do you like it strong or weak?"

"As it comes."

He watched in silence as she set the teapot on the trolley. "Let me wheel it for you."

He trundled it out and she followed him across the hall, thinking how ludicrous he looked lumbering over the squeaky old contraption. In the livingroom he sat in front of the fire and helped himself liberally to the toast.

"Damn cold coming down in the train," he said, munching heavily. "The heat was going full blast but it made no difference."

"It's always the next door carriage that's warm!"

"You've got something there." He stretched his legs to the fire and looked at her squarely. "I got your letter. That's why I came down."

She stood up nervously and reached for a cigarette. "Will you smoke?" He accepted one and lit them both in silence. "Matthew, I —" she broke off and inhaled, playing for time. "Isn't there something you want to ask me again?"

49

"If I do it will be for the last time. I said I'd ask you twice and I will, but there won't be a third time with me." He stood up and almost blocked out the fire with his bulk, his sturdy figure outlined against the glow, his blunt head thrown back. "Will you marry me, Stella?"

She took a deep breath. "Yes, Matthew, I will!"

"That's a load off my mind!"

He moved towards her, but she shook her head. "No, please sit down, I want to talk to you first."

"There's plenty of time for talking later. Anyway, I know most of the things you want to say."

"You can't."

He smiled. "I'm no fool, Stella. You want to tell me you aren't sure you love me. You also want to say that while you're not exactly marrying me for my money, you wouldn't marry me if I had nothing, and that although helping Adrian isn't a condition of marriage, if it weren't necessary to help him there'd *be* no marriage."

Aghast, she stared at him. Had she been so obvious? So easy to see through?

"Don't look so surprised," he said, "I'm a business man, Stella. I don't need to have all my t's crossed!"

Unable to stop herself she began to cry. For a few moments Matthew left her alone, then he knelt by her side and gently stroked her hair.

"Don't fret, lass, you haven't disillusioned me."

"But to think you've known all along and still want to marry me!" She cried harder but he said nothing, waiting for her to blow her nose and dry her eyes. "I'm sorry, Matthew, I must look a sight. Forgive me for making such a fool of myself."

"I'd like to think you were crying because you thought you'd made a fool of me."

The shaft went home and she bit her lip. "How can you still want me, knowing the sort of person I am?"

"I've been asking myself that ever since I met you!" His face sobered and he caught her hand. "I love you because you're honest, and one day I think you'll love me for the same reason. I don't believe you would marry a man you didn't like no matter what the circumstances were, and if you like me enough to marry me, I'm satisfied a deeper feeling will come later. A lot of marriages start off well, but the glamour doesn't last and something goes wrong. Well, there'll be no false glamour to tarnish in our marriage, and if I make you happy you'll grow to love me."

"Oh Matthew, I hope so!" She clasped her hands tight. "I'd like you to know exactly why I changed my mind. It's Adrian, as you guessed." Quickly she told him the whole story, and he heard her out in silence, not commenting until she had finished.

"Your brother's got no guts. That's his trouble. He's a snob too, and he thinks hard work is only for fools. In my book that makes him the biggest fool of the lot. If I'd wanted to study music as much as you say he does, nothing would have stopped me. But young Adrian wants everything laid on for him."

"If you think like that, you won't want to help him."

"I'll help *you*," came the answer. "And if you want him to go to the Academy, I'll foot the bill. I just want you to stop looking at him through rose-coloured glasses."

"I won't have much chance to wear them with you around!"

He half smiled. "The day you marry me, I'll settle enough on Adrian to see him through the Academy, and when he leaves I'll give him an income until he can stand on his own feet."

Too overwhelmed to speak, Stella stood up and impulsively kissed him on the cheek, but as she went to draw back he pulled her into his arms.

"I'm not your brother, you know. What about a

proper one?" His mouth closed on hers, all the pent-up longing of the weeks away from her evident in his kiss. She drew away, breathless, and he caught her hand and pressed it to his lips. "Stella, sweetheart, I've missed you so! Don't make me wait too long."

"We've only been engaged a few minutes!"

"That reminds me." He delved into his pocket and drew out a small black box. "This is for you."

She lifted the lid and a large oval diamond winked up at her like a shining eye. "I've never seen anything so beautiful!"

He looked at her as she slipped it on. "Does your mother know?"

"Know what?"

"About us. I won't ask if she approves, but does she know you're going to marry me?"

"Not yet."

"We must tell her as soon as she gets in. Is she having supper at home?"

"She's dining out."

"Beg your pardon — dinner! I can see I'll have to mind my language with you."

"Don't!" she protested. "I'll have to mind so much more! I'm sure I'll say and do things that won't fit in with your way of life, but if you're willing to show me —"

"I'll show you anything you want. You can do whatever you like as long as you marry me." He looked into her eyes. "I daren't kiss you again or we'll never get out. Let's go and celebrate."

A heavy mist prevented them going further afield than Knightsbridge, though Matthew still insisted on ordering champagne, and it was considerably later than Stella had envisaged when they returned to the flat. But despite the lateness Mrs. Percy was still not home and she suggested Matthew leave before her mother came back.

"She'll be tired and irritable," Stella said. "It will

be much better if you see her tomorrow."

"You mean you'd rather break the news to her yourself!"

Stella said nothing and he leaned forward and gently touched his lips to her cheek, the gesture showing, far more than words, that he appreciated the problem she would be facing.

Only when she was alone did Stella relax, though even this was only momentary, for she knew she could not go to bed until she had spoken to her mother. Unless she did so she would feel too guilty to sleep; more important, the longer she delayed in breaking the news, the more difficult it would become. Drawing a chair close to the fire, she waited. Time passed slowly and her eyes were drooping with fatigue when her mother came into the room.

"Good heavens, Stella, you're up late. Anything wrong?"

"No, I was waiting for you."

"It's taken me over an hour to get from Cheyne Walk. I waited ages for a taxi."

"Poor darling. Would you like a hot drink?"

"I'd love one. I'm freezing." Mrs. Percy sank into an armchair and eased her feet out of her shoes.

Returning some moments later with a steaming cup of chocolate, Stella found her mother asleep, though the blue veined lids lifted as the cup was set on the table.

A sip was appreciatively taken. "Hmm, delicious. Aren't you having any?"

"No. I had a late dinner with Matthew."

The cup clattered in the saucer. "Don't tell me *he's* in town again."

"I wish you wouldn't use that tone."

Mrs. Percy ignored the remark. "I thought you weren't going to see him again. It's obvious he's fond of you and it isn't kind to encourage him. It would be better if you refused to go out with him next time he rings up."

"I can't very well do that. We're engaged to be married."

There was a tense silence. Then Mrs. Percy gave a strained laugh. "You're joking."

"I'm not. I mean it."

"But you can't! If he's come here pestering you —"

"He didn't pester me. He asked me to marry him weeks ago and I refused. When I changed my mind I wrote and asked him to come to London."

"When you changed your —" Mrs. Percy stared at her incredulously. "You must be mad! Does Charles know?"

"No."

"Thank heavens you haven't burnt your boats! He need never know you've been such a fool."

"Mother, please! I'm engaged to Matthew and I've no intention of breaking it off. He's very wealthy — surely that pleases you?"

"I'm not in the mood for joking. How can you consider marrying a man for his money!"

"I thought you wanted me to."

"Not just *anyone* with money! If you got engaged because of some ridiculous idea of helping us, then the quicker you end it, the better! We've waited so long we can wait a little longer. Adrian's settling down nicely.

"But he isn't — that's the point. If we let him go on as he is, he'll end up in prison!"

"You don't know what you're saying!"

"Unfortunately I do. He's involved with a crowd who deal in stolen cars. That's how he's got most of the money he's been spending so freely."

"You should have told me this before. Adrian's my son and I've a right to know if he's in trouble."

"What was the point of telling you? You wouldn't have been able to do anything about it. The only hope is for him to go to the Academy; and Matthew's promised to send him there."

Mrs. Percy set her cup down sharply. "It seems that either way I shall have to sacrifice one of my children! If you don't marry this man, Adrian will end up in trouble, and if *he* has the career he wants, *you'll* be the one to suffer."

"I'm not going to suffer. I'm fond of Matthew. I know you don't like him and I agree we haven't much in common, but he's kind and he wants to make me happy."

"You haven't a hope of being happy with him! He'll insist on being master in his own home and he's too old for you to change him. You'll have to take him as you find him, manners and all, for the rest of your life."

Stella sighed. "Aren't you exaggerating? I grant he isn't as polished as the people we're used to, but then he hasn't led the same sort of life. He's made his money instead of inheriting it."

"Charles has never inherited money, but he's still a gentleman!"

"It isn't fair to compare Matthew with Charles — they're different. One's a Yorkshireman and —"

"Have you thought what *that'll* mean," her mother interrupted, "or won't you mind burying yourself in Leeds?"

The tone was so expressive that Stella smiled in spite of herself. "Leeds *is* in England, you know!"

"How can you joke about it!"

Mrs. Percy groped for her handkerchief and began to cry, and Stella knelt by her mother's chair and took her hand. "Please darling, be reasonable. Matthew's a little different but I'm sure we'll be happy. I'm not just marrying him because he can help Adrian."

"You can't love him!" Mrs. Percy cried even harder. "You're ruining your life and you can't see it. You're blind!"

"I'm not. Believe me, I know what I'm doing."

"Then your ideas have certainly altered." Mrs. Percy wiped her eyes and straightened up. "There's obviously nothing I can say to make you change your mind. It's your life and I can't stop you ruining it. But if things don't turn out as you hope, don't look to me for sympathy."

She rose, picked up her handbag and shoes and walked out of the room, leaving Stella alone by the fire.

CHAPTER SIX

STELLA was never sure whether Adrian suspected her reason for marrying Matthew, but he went out of his way to be nice to him, making up for her mother's cold unfriendliness.

She had still not broken the news to Charles, and she invited him to the flat one evening when Matthew had returned to Leeds.

She was not surprised at his reaction to the news.

"Rather sudden, isn't it?" he asked dryly. "I hadn't realized you were capable of falling in love so quickly."

"Oh Charles, don't be bitter!"

"Do you expect me to jump for joy? I've always been under the impression you were going to marry me! I know I can't support a wife yet, but —"

"That's just an excuse." Tired of pretence, Stella lost her temper. "Lots of couples marry on far less than you earn. What about milkmen or postmen — they don't go on courting for years!"

"People have different standards. Anyway, I suggested we get married several weeks ago but you —"

"You didn't mean it. If you had, you wouldn't have let me talk you out of it so easily. Be honest, Charles! If you had really loved me, you would have married me ages ago."

"Perhaps I loved you too much. I wanted things to be right for us. For us to have a home of our own and —"

"Having a house doesn't count. It's with *whom* you live that matters."

"A pity you never said this before."

"I was modest," she said bitterly. "It went against my standards!"

"So now you're dropping them completely!" Instantly he looked discomforted. "I'm sorry, Stella, I

57

had no right to say that. I've nothing against Armstrong. He seems a decent chap." Charles picked up his hat and gloves and went to the door, then with uncharacteristic impulsiveness, threw them down and strode back to her. "Break it off, Stella! You're making a mistake. Armstrong's not the man for you. You're too sensitive — too intelligent . . ."

"What about my being too selfish?" she retorted. "What makes you think I'm too good for Matthew? What about his being too good for me?"

"Don't be silly."

"Why is it silly? How do you think his friends and family will see *me*? As a spoilt fool who knows nothing about life and can't even begin to understand how hard he's worked!"

"If that's the way you feel . . ." Charles went to the door again and she made no move to stop him. "You're making a terrible mistake, Stella. You'll regret it."

"Then you'll be able to say 'I told you so!' "

"I would never gloat," he said quietly. "I love you too much for that."

Instantly her anger vanished and impulsively she reached out a hand to him. "I'm sorry, Charles, please forgive me."

"Of course I forgive you."

The room blurred as her eyes filled with tears, and when she blinked them away, he had gone.

It was not until a week before their wedding that Matthew told Stella what their home was like.

"I'm sorry I haven't any pictures of it to show you, but you'll soon be seeing it for yourself. It's a big place and not much to look at — like me — but it's practical and comfortable, with a couple of acres and a grey stone wall all round. That's where it gets it name — Grey Walls." There was satisfaction in his tone. "It's got a romantic touch that will suit you, sweetheart."

"How many rooms are there?" Stella asked, for want of something to say.

"About twelve, apart from staff quarters and such-like, with a big hall and a grand stairway. That's what I fell for when I saw the house for the first time. And by heavens, Jess was mad when I bought it just because of that!"

"Jess?"

"My sister."

"I didn't know that was her name."

"It's Jessica really, but she's always been called Jess. I hope you like her — she's the only family I have." He reached out a large hand and pulled Stella on to his lap. "At least, she was until I found you. Her husband was killed a few years ago and as she had no children she came back to look after me. Very efficient girl, our Jess — hardly a girl any longer, though it's hard for me to realize it."

"How old is she?"

"Forty-two."

"Somehow I thought she'd be in her fifties."

"Sometimes she acts like it. Never had much fun out of life, Jess hasn't. She and Tom weren't happy and she was glad to come home. She's a good house-keeper, Stella, you'll learn a thing or two from her."

"Will she go *on* living with us?"

"Yes, unless you've any objection? But you'll be in charge, and if there are any changes you want to make, just tell her."

She played with the button on his jacket. "If Jess looks after the house, it won't leave me very much to do."

"I've bought you a piano," he said casually.

For the first time her enthusiasm was spontaneous. "What a wonderful present! I dreaded having to leave mine."

"That's why I got it. Oh Stella, there's so much I want to do for you." He stroked her hair and let the palm of his hand rest on the crown of her head. "I can't think of pretty speeches or say half the things I want to say, but looking at you makes me wish I were a poet."

"Nobody's ever said anything nicer to me than that!"

Of her own accord she put her lips on his and he drew her close, his hands moving over her in a persistent caress. Their kiss lengthened and he grew less gentle, his hands so hard against her body that her desire swiftly changed to fear. With a gasp she pulled away from him and stood up.

"Matthew, don't! I — I'm not used to . . ." She clenched her hands, unaccountably near to tears.

"I'm sorry, darling." He stood behind her and encircled her waist. But now there was no passion in his touch, only tenderness. "Don't be afraid of telling me if I frighten you. I'd never do anything to hurt you."

With an effort she relaxed against him. "It's stupid of me. Forgive me for being so silly."

During the next few days they were seldom alone together, for Stella left Matthew to make all the arrangements for their wedding and honeymoon. They were to be married at St. Paul's Church, Knightsbridge, and after a small family luncheon were flying to Mombassa.

"I've wanted to see that part of Africa since I was a lad," he explained. "I hope you'll like it."

"It sounds wonderful. I haven't been abroad for years."

"Next year we can go on a cruise. That's the best way of seeing a lot of places in one go."

"I'd hate that."

"It's the only way I could do it. I can never get away for more than a couple of weeks at a time."

"Then there's no point being rich," she retorted.

60

He grinned. "You're not wrong there, lass. To begin with you make money so that you can do all the things you want, then when you've got it, you have too many responsibilities to leave them!"

She laughed. "A worried millionaire!"

"I'd be more worried if I weren't!" He looked at the travel folder in his hand. "It would have suited me to go to a quiet village somewhere, only I thought you'd prefer a bit more glamour."

Stella was touched. "You're so thoughtful and kind."

"Only to you, lass. My friends would have a fit if they heard me talk like this. I hope you like them — my friends, I mean. They're plain people, but good."

"If they're like you, I'm sure I'll like them."

He took out a cigarette and she held out her hand for one. "No, lass, you smoke too much."

"Bossing me even before we're married!" she joked, and reaching out, took a cigarette from a box on the table. "I'll just have one."

He leaned across and removed the cigarette from her lips. "Play for me, instead. I haven't heard you for weeks."

"That's not my fault. You've been so busy dashing between London and Leeds that I've hardly seen you."

"There's quite a bit to do, one way and the other. We'll be away a month and there's some trouble at one of the factories I'd like to settle before we go."

"What sort of trouble?"

"A strike threat. But don't bother your pretty head about it. When I'm with you I want to forget business. Give us a bit of music."

The phraseology jarred, but she strove to ignore it. "Anything in particular?"

He hummed a few bars. "What about that? I don't know what it's called, but it's one of my favourites."

"Clair de Lune."

Her hands moved over the keys in Debussy's

haunting melody and Matthew sat back and watched her with pride, enjoying the lovely picture she made in the pale room with the dark piano forming a black-and-white background to the vivid garnet of her dress.

Stella played almost without thinking, her eyes bent over the keyboard, her expression serious as she drifted from 'Clair de Lune' into 'Greensleeves,' running through the words in her mind as she struck the notes.

> 'Alas, my love, you do me wrong
> To cast me off discourteously,
> For I have loved you so long,
> Delighting in your company.'

Unbidden, the thought of Charles came into her mind. He had loved her long and delighted in her company, but his delight had been so tame that she had felt it was indeed no more than discourtesy to have cast him off.

> 'For oh! Greensleeves is my delight
> And oh, Greensleeves is all my joy,
> And oh! Greensleeves is my heart of gold,
> My lovely Lady Greensleeves.'

Now she was to be Matthew's delight, all his joy, his heart of gold.

The last note died away and she turned and looked at him. He had fallen asleep, his head resting against the cushion, his arms hanging limply at his sides. With a smile she moved over and looked at him. He must be tired after the effort of trying to finish so much work in such a short time. This marriage meant a great deal to him — he had waited so long before taking a wife that he deserved much more than she could offer. Gently she touched his hair, turned off the light and tiptoed out of the room.

Stella married Matthew early one raw morning in February with only Adrian and her mother as witnesses. As Matthew repeated his vows his deep voice faltered, and for the first time she understood the depth of his feeling for her. It was strange that he should give rise to such different emotions in her — one moment affection, the next irritation. Perhaps when they were alone together, when she was no longer conscious of Adrian's speculative amusement and her mother's acid disparagement, they would reach a real understanding.

During luncheon at the Ritz Matthew seemed impervious to his mother-in-law's coldness, chipping Adrian and looking at Stella with such adoration that she longed to beg him not to love her so much. The meal had to be a brief one, for their plane was due to leave in the early afternoon, and as soon as they had finished eating she glanced at the diamond watch he had given her as a wedding present, and saw they had only an hour to get to the airport.

"We haven't much time, Matthew."

His reply was forestalled by the approach of a waiter to say he was wanted on the telephone. "It must be Jess, I bet she's sorry she didn't come down after all."

"Why didn't she?" Adrian asked Stella when Matthew had left the table.

"I don't know," Stella replied, "And I didn't think it wise to ask!"

"Looks as if you might have a sister-in-law instead of mother-in-law trouble."

"Thanks," Stella said dryly.

"Sometimes you talk too much," Mrs. Percy said to her son, and then looked at Stella. "I do hope you put on some weight while you're on holiday. You're too thin."

It was the first sign of concern her mother had shown, and Stella was touched. "Don't worry about me, darling, I feel fine."

"You don't look it. If only —" Mrs. Percy stopped as Matthew returned to the table, his expression concerned.

"It was my manager," he said, "there's a strike at one of the factories and I've got to get up there."

"You're joking!" Stella gasped.

"I wish to heaven I were, but a thousand men have walked out."

"Can't someone else deal with it?"

"I'm the only person who can handle it now."

"But what about our honeymoon? You can't go back!"

"I'm sorry, lass, but we must. The train leaves King's Cross in twenty minutes. I'll see to our luggage."

He hurried away and Mrs. Percy flung down her napkin. "I've never heard anything so ridiculous. What does he employ a manager for?" Her face crumpled and she began to cry. "He doesn't consider your feelings at all. All he cares about is business."

"Please, Mother, crying won't help."

"Nothing will help you now. Your life's ruined!" With an effort Mrs. Percy controlled herself. "What will it be like in Leeds? No one's expecting you and the house won't even be prepared."

"The strikers will give 'em a warm reception," Adrian quipped.

"This is no time for facetiousness," his mother said sharply.

"Sorry, Ma, I was only trying to cheer you up." He looked at his sister. "We can telephone Jess and let her know you're coming."

"Perhaps you'd better," Stella said dully, and pushed back her chair as Matthew appeared, his coat over his arm.

A month earlier than she had anticipated, Stella found herself on the train to Leeds. It was too crowded for them to find seats together, and they sat at opposite ends of the carriage. What a way to start a marriage, she though bitterly. Instead of arriving in a warm,

64

sunny climate, she would soon be in the bleak coldness of the moors, in a strange house with a strange woman in command. The resentment she had tried to control, increased with every mile, and at four o'clock, when Matthew asked if she would like some tea, she followed him to the restaurant car without a word.

Even here there was no vacant table and they had to wait outside, swaying as the train lurched over the rails, cold gusts of wind coming at them with every creak and rattle.

By the time they were shown to a table she was almost speechless with cold, and Matthew looked at her in concern. "A cup of tea will warm you up, sweetheart. You should have put on a thicker dress."

"I didn't expect to need it in Africa!"

He reached for her hand but she withdrew it quickly. "Stella, try and understand why I have to get back. Some of these men have worked for me twenty years, I couldn't let 'em down."

"So you let me down instead!"

"I'm sorry, lass. As soon as this business is settled we'll go away for as long as you like."

She averted her face and they finished their tea in silence. Back in the compartment she dozed intermittently, waking up to find the train drawing into Leeds station. Hastily she powdered her nose and a few minutes later was walking down the platform to the barrier.

"There's Ted!" Stella followed Matthew's gaze to a tall, thin man making his way towards them.

"Hullo, Matt! Glad your train's on time. And this'll be Mrs. Armstrong?" He shook Stella's hand vigorously. "Welcome home! I hope you'll be very happy."

Her reply was drowned by the shriek of a train whistle and the manager turned to Matthew.

"Good thing you came back right away. They're in

the middle of a meeting and you ought to get there before it's over."

"I suppose Parker's behind it?"

"Plus a few new ones. If you can talk to the men before they pass any resolution, you —"

"Then we'd better not waste time," Matthew interrupted and swung round to Stella. "I'm sorry, lass, but I can't take you home."

"I reckoned on that," Ted intervened, "and I've laid on two cars. Bob can take Mrs. Armstrong home. Bob's my son," he explained to Stella.

She was too taken aback to speak, and sensing it Matthew drew her to one side. "Try and understand sweetheart. If I can talk to the men before they pass any resolution, I might be able to persuade them to go back."

"Don't worry about me," she said frigidly. "I can manage to introduce myself to your sister."

He led her into the station yard where several cars were parked, and a young man standing beside a Rolls Royce came forward to greet them.

Hurriedly Matthew saw Stella into the back seat. "Bob will drive you straight home. Tell Jess I'll try and get back by eight. If I'm not, don't wait supper."

He hurried away and Stella blinked her eyes, close to tears.

"This your first time in Leeds, Mrs. Armstrong?" Bob asked as he set the car in motion.

"Yes."

"It'll take a bit of getting used to after London."

She murmured a non committal reply and the young man lapsed into silence as they drove through Chapel Town and beyond Alwoodley, following the main road until he slackened speed and swung into a half moon drive to stop at a large, front door.

By now it was dark and Stella could scarcely see as she mounted the steps and knocked. Footsteps sounded and the door opened to reveal a tall, big-boned woman.

"Is that you, Matt?"

"No, it's — I'm Stella." She moistened her lips. "Matthew's gone to a meeting and sent me on."

The woman stood back. "Come on in. I'm Jess."

Stella stepped into a dark panelled hall with a preponderance of black doors, the only feature in it's favour a beautifully carved oak staircase that led to the first floor.

"Bring the cases in the front way, Bob, they'll be too heavy to lug round the back. Then go through and have a cup o'tea. I've just made some." Jess closed the door and appraised Stella for a moment. "I'd better show you to your room, you'll be wanting to have a wash. Will Matt be in for supper?"

"He said he'd try to get back by eight."

"Good. Your brother telephoned me you were coming, so I just had time to put your room to rights. We weren't expecting you, so there's not much food in the house. When I'm alone I don't bother with cooking."

"Are you on your own, then?"

"We've one maid," Jess said briefly and led the way up the stairs into a large bedroom filled with dark furniture. A heavy walnut wardrobe, dressing-table and tallboy were ranged round the walls and there was a wide double bed covered with a pale blue brocade bedspread that matched the curtains hanging stiffly at the tall window.

"This is Matt's room," the woman said. "That door leads to the bathroom and the one over there is the dressing-room. I'll leave you to get settled. You'll find me in the front room. That's the second door on the right as you come down."

She went out and Stella sank on to the bed, filled with desolation. What was she doing here among these strangers? What had she in common with that brusque woman and the man who was to come back to her tonight? For the first time she realized the irrevocable step she had taken and wished with all her heart that Matthew was here to dispel her fears.

Longing for the warmth and shabby cheerfulness of the flat in Knightsbridge, she started to unpack, hanging her clothes beside Matthew's in the enormous wardrobe before she went down to the drawing-room. For a moment she hesitated outside the door, then turned the handle and went in. Her sister-in-law was sitting behind a tea-trolley by the fire.

"You've been quick." She picked up a china teapot. "Thought you might like a cup of tea. How do you take it?"

"Fairly weak, please."

Stella looked round the room as she sipped. Everything was in ornate bad taste, from the gilded wall brackets writhing on the wall to the gaudy Turkish carpet. Against the far wall stood a bookcase, the shelves filled with cheap book-club editions, while along the other wall an imitation antique cocktail cabinet vied for pride of place with a rosewood baby grand. Ranged around the rest of the room was a dull green Knowle suite, the high-backed chairs stiff and uncomfortable.

Noticing her appraisal of the room, Jess smiled. "Matt made me redecorate for you."

"It's very nice," Stella lied.

Jess picked up a sock she had been mending. "Must have been a disappointment to miss your honeymoon. But business means a lot to Matt — if it hadn't, he wouldn't be where he is today. I was surprised when he told me he was going to wed. He's been a bachelor so long I never thought he'd change."

She lowered the sock and leaned forward, but although she was smiling Stella felt no response. The big mouth and fleshy nose made the woman's face heavy and masculine, while her sallow skin was marred by moles that stuck out on the lower half of her face like pebbles on a sandy beach. Brown eyes were marked by thick brows, and the dark hair was cut in a travesty of current fashion, giving her head the aspect of a misshapen egg. As she stood up to refill Stella's cup her large hands and feet made her seem bigger than she was, the brown wool dress failing to disguise the thickness of her body and the full, heavy bosom.

"What did you do before your marriage?"

"Nothing."

"Didn't you find it boring? I know I would have done."

"Do you work, then?" Stella asked, surprised.

"Keeping house is a full time job."

"I kept house too," Stella said quickly.

"A flat." The work was dismissed. *This* house is different. Folk coming and going at all hours of the day and night and maids walking out when the fancy takes them. I suppose they're just as high-handed in London?"

"I don't know. We only have a daily once a week."

"Of course. Matt said you were poor."

Stella flushed. "Not everyone's as lucky as your brother."

"Your husband, you mean. And it wasn't luck; it was hard work. That's why I take care of his money. And I hope you'll do the same. I believe in calling a spade a spade, and if we're going to get on together we might as well know where we stand from the start. I've made this my home since my husband was killed and I've put a lot of work into it."

"Matthew's told me how well you manage the house," Stella said quietly, "and I certainly don't mind if you'd like to go on doing it."

"That's one thing settled." The woman relaxed in her chair. "You aren't what I expected. Not Matt's type at all."

Stella forced a smile. "What type did you expect?"

"Someone more full-blooded. No offence meant, of course. Still, they always say men are attracted to their opposites."

"Was your husband like you?"

"Lord no! Better looking, with black hair and blue eyes. Not much backbone though. A weak man, you could say."

"It's no good having more than one boss in a marriage."

"You're right there," Jess grunted, "but every woman wants to be bossed sometimes. No matter how capable you are, you like to feel you can lean on your man occasionally without him falling down."

Diplomatically Stella remained silent and her sister-in-law bit off a strand of wool and stood up. "I'll see about supper. Perhaps you'll finish this sock — it's your husband's."

She walked out and Stella looked at the sock help-lessly. A large hole had been partially filled in and she took up the needle and began to darn. A second later she dropped it with a sharp exclamation. A bubble of blood was widening at her finger-tip and she wiped it on her handkerchief, thinking wryly that she had a lot to learn before she could compete with Matthew's sister.

Adrian's last words came into her mind, and she wondered what he would have said if he had over-heard her encounter with Jess. A sister-in-law instead of a mother-in-law. And what a sister-in-law. She shivered and wished with all her heart that Matthew were here. Only when he came would she lose the fear that was threatening to overwhelm her. Jumping to her feet, she went upstairs to change into her pret-tiest dress. After all, this *was* her wedding day!

CHAPTER SEVEN

STELLA hoped that Matthew would not add insult to injury by being late for dinner, and as she entered the drawing room, Jess's comment did nothing to decrease her apprehension.

"You're all dressed up for just the two of us. What's the occasion?"

"My first dinner at home with my husband," Stella said.

"I doubt if he'll turn up. Many's the time I've sat and waited while the food's spoilt."

"I don't think he'll be late tonight."

"I hope you're right. He'll like your dress — blue's one of his favourite colours, but I suppose you knew that."

"I didn't, as a matter of fact." Stella sat down. "I don't know much about his tastes. You must tell me."

"You'll find out soon enough." Jess smoothed the brown dress over her knees. "I've not changed, but he's used to seeing me the way I am. My husband never bothered how I looked." She glanced at her watch. "I thought you said Matt would be home at eight? It's nearly quarter past — do you want to start?"

"I'd like to wait a little longer."

"Suits me. We've only hot-pot. Sorry it's not more fancy, but by the time your brother rang the shops were shut. Still, there's sherry trifle for dessert — it's Matt's favourite."

The two women lapsed into a silence only broken by the crackling of the fire and the ticking of the clock, and Stella racked her brains for something to say, relieved when Jess stood up.

"It's half past; we'd better sit down. Elsie has to get the washing-up done."

She led the way into the dining-room, jerking her thumb behind her as she went. "That door leads to the hall and takes you to the kitchen, the scullery and Matt's hideout."

"His what?"

"Study I suppose *you'd* call it."

Stella did not reply and looked curiously round the dining-room. Unlike the room they had just vacated it was fairly modern, with a long table and a sideboard supporting two silver candlesticks. Here too an inferior Turkish carpet decorated the floor, the colours at variance with the window-length curtains. Pride of place above the mantelpiece was given to a painting of waxy-looking flowers from which she hastily averted her eyes.

Jess pointed. "You'd better sit next to the fire. You look frozen."

As Stella sat down a plump, fair-haired maid came in with a brown casserole.

Jess heaped a plate and passed it over. "Here, put this inside you while it's hot."

Stella looked at the steaming mass, picked up her fork and with an effort began to eat.

They had almost finished their first course when the front door slammed and Matthew strode into the room. He enveloped Stella in a bear-like hug, the dampness of his coat striking so cold that she drew away.

"Matthew, you're frozen!"

"I know." He pulled off his gloves. "Sorry we're late. Hullo, Jess."

"Hullo, Matt. Did the meeting go all right?"

"So-so. I'm seeing the leaders in the morning to try and reach an agreement." He slapped her on the back. "Didn't think you'd be seeing me home so soon, eh? Still, I'll not be long settling things, then Stella and I will be off."

There was a step behind him and Ted Robbins

came apologetically into the room. "Sorry to trouble you, Jess, but I'm here too."

She grunted and went out, and Stella looked from the manager to Matthew. "I thought the meeting was over."

"So it is. But there's another one in the morning, and Ted and I have got to work out what to say."

"Must you do it tonight?" she asked icily.

"Can't be helped, sweetheart." He sat at the table and reached for a slice of bread. "Lord, I'm starving! Never could stand the tea you get on trains. Not enough to fill a fly's belly!"

He went on talking but Stella did not listen, too intent on fighting back her tears.

Jess returned with another casserole and the two men ate hurriedly and in silence, Ted nervously crumbling his bread and glancing occasionally at Stella. When they had finished, Jess put plates of trifle in front of them and as soon as Matthew had swallowed the last mouthful he stood up.

"Let's get cracking, Ted. I want to finish early."

The manager rose and Jess started stacking the plates. "Go into the front room, Stella. I won't be long."

"Can I help?" Stella offered.

Matthew turned at the door. "Jess can manage." He waited for Stella to precede him into the hall. "Go into the den, Ted. I want a word with my wife."

He followed Stella into the drawing-room and went to take her in his arms. "Give us a kiss, sweetheart."

She pulled angrily away from him and knelt in front of the fire. "Aren't you wasting time? I thought you had to talk to your manager."

"Don't be angry with me, darling. I'd have given anything in the world for this not to have happened. Especially today! But I had no choice. I *had* to come back."

"You put your business before me!"

"Don't be silly. You know how I feel about you. But I couldn't leave it to Ted. If anything goes wrong at *this* factory, it could be serious." He tilted her face and placed a kiss on her brow. "I hate leaving you, darling. I'll be as quick as I can."

"I couldn't care less," she retorted. "My whole day's been ruined anyway."

He looked at her helplessly, then with a shake of his head, walked out of the room.

The rest of the evening was a repetition of the afternoon. Jess sat stolidly in front of the fire, and Stella found conversation so difficult that she was thankful when at half past eleven her sister-in-law folded her knitting and stood up.

"I'm off to bed. I'm up at six in the morning."

"Are you going out?"

Jess looked surprised. Then she smiled loftily. "I'm always up at six. I worked in a mill when I was a girl and old habits die hard."

"Surely you like to lie in. occasionally?"

"Never. There'll be plenty of time for resting when I'm dead!"

On this cheerful note she departed, and Stella drew closer to the fire. More than ever she felt a stranger here, with no affinity to the house or it's occupants. The man whose muffled voice she could hear across the hall was her husband, but she felt no warmth towards him, only hurt and disappointment. She had known their outlook was different, but had been sure they would find some mutual understanding on which to base their marriage. His behaviour today had proved her wrong, for in her wildest imaginings she had not foreseen a wedding day like this.

The clock chiming midnight roused her from her thoughts and with an exclamation she went upstairs. The bed had been turned down at both sides and she avoided looking at it as she undressed. Even a hot

74

bath did not ease her tension, and she trembled with humiliation and fatigue.

At one o'clock she was lying in bed staring at the ceiling. With every passing moment her body grew more rigid, but the clock had chimed two before she heard Matthew's step on the stair.

Gently the handle turned and Stella closed her eyes, her heart beating heavily as she felt him approach the bed and look at her before he made his way to the dressing-room. Doors opened and closed, a wardrobe squeaked and there was a muttered oath, then he went into the bathroom and she heard the sound of running water.

When he came back her eyes were open, and he smiled and sat on the edge of the bed, unfamiliar in a dark green dressing-gown.

"Hullo, sweetheart," he said softly. "Sorry I'm late."

"I thought you weren't coming to bed at all!"

"On my wedding night?" There was a hint of laughter in his voice and he leaned across and stroked her arm. "Don't be upset, Stel. I couldn't help it."

"Is that going to be your excuse for everything?"

"Please darling, try and understand. This sort of thing happens once in a lifetime." He took her in his arms. "I've waited so long to hold you like this, don't spoil it now. Why sweetheart, you're shivering — you're cold as ice!" He rested his cheek against her hair. "I love you so much. I can't bear you to be angry."

Tenderly he kissed the hollow of her throat, his hands clumsily playing with the frail straps of her night-dress. "Sweetheart," he muttered thickly, "I love you." Pulling her closer still he pressed his lips to the swelling curve of her breasts. He was breathing heavily, his words incoherent as he savoured the smooth coolness of her skin, so soft against his own, so dry against the dampness of his brow. His hands

75

were more insistent now, their touch firmer, demanding, moving with the assurance of possession along her waist and down her thighs.

In an agony of mortification Stella stared into the darkness, hating her body for its abandoned response, hating Matthew for his assumption that he could leave her alone for hours and then come and possess her as though it were his divine right. How dare he touch her like this! How dare he put his hands — his mouth —

"No!" she screamed. "Don't touch me!" Like a wild cat she tore away from him and slithered to the other side of the bed. "Leave me alone," she panted. "I can't bear you!"

"Darling, you're upset. You don't mean it."

"I mean every word! Do you think you can make love to me when it suits you? That I can wait until there's nothing better for you to do? I'm a woman Matthew, not a statue!"

"You're upset, sweetheart. If —"

"Upset sweetheart," she mimicked. "Is that the only word in your vocabulary. Of course I'm upset! Upset that I was stupid enough to marry you! Stupid enough to think we could ever be happy together."

"You don't know what you're saying!"

"I do! I do! You're selfish and inconsiderate and — and common!" She tossed her head. "That's what you are — clumsy and common!" Her face crumpled and she buried her head in her arms, her thin shoulders shaking with sobs. "You leave me alone all day and half the night and then expect me to — to . . . and I can't," she cried. "I can't! Go away and leave me alone."

The bed creaked as he stood up. "There's no need to cry. You've nothing to be afraid of. I won't come near again unless you ask me."

Her sobs grew deeper; for herself, for him, for

76

both their shattered dreams. "Matthew," she gasped, and lifted her head.

But he was gone.

Lying wakeful throughout the night Stella faced the knowledge that her outburst had brought into the open a fact which she had even been hiding from herself: though she found Matthew attractive, his personal mannerisms and speech jarred on her so forcibly that it destroyed her desire for him. Had Charles acted in the same way — putting an important case before his honeymoon — would she have been so angry? In all honesty she knew the answer was no, and acknowledging this, she wondered dismally where she and Matthew could go from here. If only she had realised her true feelings for him before she had become his wife! Yet during their engagement she had thought her fear of his lovemaking the natural reaction of an inexperienced girl against the ardour of a mature and passionate man. She had hoped that once they were married, her liking for him would make a normal relationship possible.

Now she knew this was out of the question. Any happiness they might achieve would have to be worked for by both of them. But could Matthew forgive her outburst of last night? Could he forget the wounding things she had said?

Slowly the darkness limped it's way to dawn, and as her watch showed seven, she put on her dressing-gown and went across to the dressing-room. There was no reply when she knocked on the door, and she went in hesitantly to find Matthew still in bed, his face flushed from sleep, his hair awry.

He regarded her in silence and she sat on the end of his bed and hid her trembling hands in her lap.

"I — I want to apologise for last night," she whispered. "If I could take back what I said . . . make you forget it . . ."

"I can't forget," he said huskily.

"But if you could at least understand . . ." She went over to the window, heedless of the cold wind blowing in on her. "If only you'd know what it was like for me to be here . . . alone in this house . . . feeling like a stranger . . . unwanted — in the way . . . and then having to wait up for you — knowing you weren't even thinking of me until you came in and saw me in bed!" Her voice cracked but she forced herself to continue. "I'm not making excuses for what I said. I'll hate myself for it for the rest of my life." She swung round and forced herself to look at him. "That's what I want you to know. That I'd give anything in the world if I could turn back the clock — if I could have the last few hours over again."

"I wish it too," he said heavily, "but we can't. And there's no use fretting about it." He patted the side of the bed. "Come and sit here, Stella, you'll catch your death of cold by the window."

Close to him she saw that his eyes were dull, as if he too had been awake for most of the night. The stubble on his cheeks and chin showed dark against the whiteness of his pillow and he looked tired and defeated.

"I can understand you not wanting me to touch you last night. When a woman's hurt, it's her first reaction. But I can't forget what you said. I didn't even know you thought them."

"I'm sorry," she repeated miserably.

"I daresay you are. But I'll not keep any woman against her will."

"Matthew, don't! I've tried to explain. Can't you understand?"

"I understand too well. Not that I blame you," he went on. "If we'd gone on our honeymoon none of this might have happened. In Africa I'd have been an Englishman abroad; but in England itself I'm a foreigner to you — a stranger with whom you've nothing in common. To understand me, you've got to learn another language — but it's a language you despise. You made that abundantly clear."

"I despise *myself*," she protested, "not you."

"You say that *now* — because you're sorry for me. But deep down — in your heart — it's what you really think of me."

"No!"

"Yes," he contradicted. "You do. I must have been blind not to have seen it for myself." He gave a harsh laugh. "Blind or in love. It amounts to the same thing!" He leaned against his pillow, talking half to himself, half to her. "I knew you were critical of me — some of the things I said grated on you — I could tell from the way you sometimes looked at me. But I didn't think it mattered. Lots of people from different backgrounds are happily married. Their love helps them to meet each other halfway, I suppose. Our problem is that *you* don't love me. That's why I irritate you."

"You make me sound an awful prig."

"You are! But I thought we'd overcome it." He smiled, slightly amused at her look of surprise. "Many things you do irritate *me*. You never thought of that, did you?"

She shook her head. "What sort of things?"

"*Your* way of speaking, for one. All stiff upper lip and politeness. And the way you're always so formal and reserved. But I love you in spite of it. In your case, you love me less."

Chastened, she looked away from him. "If we get used to each other perhaps —"

"I won't change," he said forcefully, "and neither will you. It's just whether or not you can accept me as I am."

"I want to!" Bursting into tears, she fell on her knees beside the bed. "I want to, Matthew, but you must help me."

"I am as I am. I can't change."

"Then *I* will. But give me time."

"As much as you want." He tenderly stroked her cheek, waiting until her sobs had subsided before he spoke again. "Go and rest, Stella. You look tired."

"So do you." Wiping her eyes she stood up. "I hope you — you won't tell your sister about last night. I don't want anyone to know."

"You've no fear of that. It's not something I'm likely to boast about!"

Tears filled her eyes again, and overcome by self-loathing she closed the door and went back to bed.

Matthew had accepted her apology — had even acted as though he understood the reason for her behaviour — but this in no way lessened the pain she had caused him, nor eased the bitterness he must feel when he remembered her wounding remarks. Only when she could love him properly, when she could hold him in her arms and return his passion, would he forget her taunts.

"Let me love him soon," she prayed. "Let me love him the way he deserves." With these words on her lips she fell asleep, not waking till the maid came in with her breakfast. Watery sunshine seeped through the curtains, lightening the heavy furniture, and though the room was still sombre there was nothing sinister about it in the light of day.

Stella sat up. "Good morning, Elsie."

" 'Morning, Mrs. Matthew. You'd best cover up a bit. It's colder here than down south."

"My bed-jacket's in the top drawer. Would you get it for me?"

The girl did as she was told. "My, what pretty things! Which one do you want?"

"The blue one's the warmest."

Elsie brought it over and put the tray on the bedside table. "Hope you manage to get all this inside you!"

Stella looked in dismay at a bowl of porridge, a

kipper and a pile of toast. "I'm afraid I don't eat half of it — I'm not used to more than toast and coffee and fruit juice."

"You'll not get fruit here in winter. Miss Jess says it's too dear for squeezing."

"I'll have to see what I can do," Stella smiled and changed the subject. "Have you been here long?"

"A year. There used to be another girl but she only stayed a few months. I give Miss Jess as good as she gives me and no offence, but anyone with a weak will can't work for her." The pale eyes crinkled. "I'd better go, or she'll be after me for wasting time."

Left alone, Stella picked at her breakfast. Although she had agreed to leave the housekeeping in her sister-in-law's hands, there were several innovations she would make. Jess must not be misled into taking what she had said last night too literally. As Matthew had said, there could be only one mistress of Grey Walls.

After breakfast she made a tour of the house. There were eight main bedrooms, all furnished in heavy wood and dark colours, as well as a large playroom with a service lift that led down to the kitchen, and she wondered with a pang whether Matthew had intended it as the nursery quarters.

Down in the hall once more she gave a cursory glance into the drawing-room before opening the door to Matthew's study, surprised to find it light and modern. Two walls were lined by bookcases filled with leather-bound editions of the classics, while a smaller bookcase stood behind the maple desk, the volumes technical and much more well thumbed.

She debated whether to go in search of Jess, and after a moment's hesitation pushed open one of the doors and found herself in a rectangular kitchen on one side of which was a sitting-room and on the other a scullery.

Jess was by the stove. "So you're down. Matt said you would be staying in bed all morning. If I'd known you weren't, I wouldn't have sent up your breakfast."

"I like it in bed anyway, thanks."

Jess grunted. "You'll be lucky if you get Elsie to climb the stairs with a heavy tray every morning. It's a big enough house for one to manage as it is."

"I agree." Stella perched on the kitchen table. "Don't you think we should advertise for someone else — or perhaps even a couple? The woman could do the cooking and the man —"

"Matt won't have a man around his house! He's not the type to put up with a butler."

"He needn't be a butler — more of an odd-job man. He could wait at table and polish the silver and —"

"Bit of an expense to have a man for that."

"He would find more to do once he started," Stella said pleasantly. "If you could tell me what paper to advertise in, we could work out what to say between us."

Jess's face was red with anger as she turned from the stove. "You're taking a great deal on yourself, aren't you? You've only been here a few hours and you want to change everything! You agreed to let me run the house —"

"As long as I have a say in it."

"It's more than a say you're wanting, by the sound of it."

"Not at all. I just think you're more economical than you need be."

"You know a good deal after one day, don't you?" Jess's voice was strident. "I'll thank you to let me mind my business and you mind yours."

"But it is my business!"

"Matt's never complained. We may not be as fancy as you, but we know how to live even if we don't use finger bowls! Matt had to slave for years to get where he is now, and I'm not having a chit of a girl spend all the money he's worked so hard to earn!"

Stella was aghast at the tirade she had evoked. In a good humour her sister-in-law was none too pleasant, but in a rage she was even more unprepossessing. "There's no point in discussing it any more, Jess. If you have anything else to say, you'd better say it to Matthew."

"I certainly will."

Still shaken by the scene, Stella took refuge in the garden. No one had ever spoken to her so belligerently, and it was several minutes before her annoyance had cooled sufficiently for her to become aware of her surroundings.

As Matthew had said, the land at the back of the house was extensive, with wide lawns bordered by beech trees and firs. Strolling along one side of a grass verge that led to a small pond, she saw a large bush of wintersweet, the long sprigs laden with such lovely maroon and yellow flowers that she would have liked to take some back to the house, reluctantly deciding not to in case it gave Jess another cause for complaint.

For half an hour she wandered the gravel paths, finally driven indoors by the cold. In the drawing-room the fire was laid but unlit, and she pressed the bell by the mantelpiece.

After a moment Jess appeared in the doorway. "Was it you on the bell?"

"Yes. I wanted Elsie to light the fire."

Her sister-in-law stumped over to the grate, and taking a box of matches from the pocket of her apron, set light to the paper and wood. "You'll find matches in the cabinet over there. We've never made a practice of ringing for maids to do our work."

Jess walked out, and Stella sat down and warmed her hands. Her sister-in-law was going to be more difficult to get on with than she had imagined. She would leave Matthew to deal with her.

To Stella's chagrin he seemed reluctant to do so

when she tackled him a few days later. Throughout the week she tried to hide her irritation that Jess never left them alone together, equally irritated with Matthew for not showing he wanted his bride to himself; how did he expect her to get to know him if there was always a third person present? But tonight Jess was out, and though it seemed a pity to bring up a subject which was bound to lead to controversy, unless she took the opportunity it might be some time before they were on their own again.

As soon as they finished dinner and went into the drawing-room she took the plunge. "I think we ought to have more help in the house, Matthew."

"Do you? It's always been enough in the past."

"This house is too big to be run by one maid," she persisted.

"Jess has never complained."

"I know, but I don't agree with the way she manages."

"How d'you mean?"

"Well, for one thing I'd like breakfast in my room every morning, or at least have it in the dining-room and not the kitchen. And for another, I'd like someone to wait at table. I know Elsie brings the food in, but she can't be expected to hand it round when she has the dishing-up and everything else in the kitchen to cope with."

"We never stand on ceremony here."

"It's hardly standing on ceremony to follow a few simple conventions of good living! After all, you can afford it!"

He stood up and knocked his pipe out against the mantelpiece. "I'll have a word with Jess and see what she says. But I don't want to go over her head." He sat down again. "Now come over here — I haven't seen much of you the last few days."

She brushed this aside. "What do you mean, go over Jess's head? You told me I could alter anything

I didn't like. It's not as if I'm suggesting increasing your sister's work — far from it —. it would give her more spare time."

He smiled. "What would Jess be doing with spare time? I know you want everything to be nice, but try to be tactful where she's concerned. She's rather sensitive, you know."

"Sensitive is a word I'd never apply to her!"

"You can't go by appearances, Stella — you should know that by now. Jess has worked very hard —"

"That's just my point, Matthew — too hard when there's been no need for it. I could understand if she wanted to save money, but she can have as much help as she wanted. The fact that she hasn't, is because she's mean!"

"If you've come up the hard way like we have, you don't throw your money around," he said quietly.

"But *you're* not mean, Matthew, and you're the one who works for the money!"

"Women often find it more difficult to change their habits."

"I only want to improve the way we live." Stella forced herself to speak quietly. "You work extremely hard, and your life could be made easier and pleasanter."

"My life's just the way I like it — or almost."

The implication did not go unnoticed, and she accepted the challenge. "Perhaps I've no right to alter things here. I'm not your wife in the real sense and —"

"I wasn't meaning that! You've every right to alter things. The house *could* do with improving, and there's no reason why Jess shouldn't take it easy. But let me tell her in my own way."

"Don't let her talk you out of it."

"There's no fear of that. I can be obstinate too! Now come close. It's the first time we've been alone for weeks."

"I didn't think you'd noticed."

"You'd be surprised what I notice. I'm not as insensitive as you —"

"Don't!" she pleaded. "Can't you forget what I said that night?"

"I'm doing my best," he said quietly.

She caught his hand and pressed it to her face. "Oh Matthew . . . be patient with me."

"As patient as I can. But I love you so much that sometimes it's difficult not to . . . Well, no more of this talk. Let's switch to politics. It'll be safer!"

CHAPTER EIGHT

FEBRUARY gave way to March, but the weather did not improve, and the icy cold was driven into the house by fierce winds from the moors.

To Stella's dismay Matthew said nothing to Jess about the running of the house, and she was forced to conclude he was afraid of upsetting his sister. But what about upsetting his wife? How did he expect them to establish a relationship when he made no effort to help her feel she belonged to his home?

Everything was run the way Jess dictated. And what a dictator she was. Deliberately she went out of her way to make Stella feel an intruder. Fires were never lit till mid-afternoon, hot water was kept at a low temperature until Matthew was due home, and many of the meals comprised food which she knew Stella did not like, turning up again cold at the next day's lunch table.

Even on a limited budget in London, Stella had managed a more varied economy, and fruit and prime cuts of meat had never been as rare in the Kensington flat as they were at Grey Walls.

With nothing to do all day, time dragged. Playing the piano did not occupy her for long, and she would wander from room to room visualizing how she would improve them if she were given a free hand. But at least foliage did not cost money when there was a large garden from which to pick it, and one morning she asked Jess for some vases.

"What do you want them for?"

"To put some leaves in."

"Bit expensive to buy greenery this time of year. Expecting visitors?"

"I don't buy flowers to impress visitors. As it so happens, I thought we'd use what's in the garden."

Jess grunted. "No point cluttering the house with mucky leaves."

"I'd still like some vases. If you'll tell me where they are . . ."

"Don't bother," Jess said grudgingly. "I'll get 'em for you."

Stella walked out of the house with a sigh of relief. It would be ironical if she could not find anything to pick after all! But the garden was full of foliage and she was surprised at the growth beginning to unfold in the cold winter air. Large bunches of flowering cherry raised frail white wands to the sky, and she had picked several budding sprays before she became aware of a wizened old man watching her.

She smiled at him. "You must be the gardener. I'm Mrs. Armstrong."

"I know. I've seen you walking around. You picked nothing, though."

"I'd like something now. The house needs brightening."

" 'Tis time my work was appreciated," he said heavily. "Tell me what you want and I'll pick it."

"I'll leave it to you. But enough for several vases."

Smiling her thanks she wandered slowly back and, wiping the mud off her shoes, went into the kitchen to find her sister-in-law rolling some pastry. "Vases are in the scullery," she said brusquely, "and Albert's left flowers there too. Enough to sink a ship."

Ignoring this pleasantry, Stella set to work, filling vases and carrying them one by one into the hall, drawing-room and dining-room. At least the rooms would not look so bare when they had guests.

In front of outsiders Jess assumed an air of friendliness towards her sister-in-law, and Stella was aware that she was considered extremely lucky to have such a capable person to manage the house for her. She also suspected that she was the subject of much discussion, and felt that whatever criticisms were made would not fall on deaf ears, for Jess's friends seemed to regard her with mistrust.

Matthew was well liked and they received many invitations to dinner or card evenings, which Stella found extremely tedious. She had never learned Bridge or Canasta and had such a poor card sense that although she accepted Matthew's offer to teach her, it was obviously such a penance that he gave it up.

Matthew's closest friends, Milly and Ned Barrett, were abroad when Stella arrived at Grey Walls, but as soon as they returned Milly telephoned, and Stella immediately liked the warm voice which welcomed her to Yorkshire, and invited her and Matthew to dine. Certain the party would not be a fashionable one, she took care not to overdress, and went down to join Matthew feeling that in her simple olive green dress she would not be accused of trying to create an impression.

To her surprise Jess was elaborately coiffeured and gowned: her hair a mass of tight waves, her ungainly figure encased in black velvet whose lustre highlighted every bulge.

"*You* didn't bother much, did you?" Jess commented as Stella reached the hall.

Biting back a sharp reply, Stella glanced at Matthew, but he looked at her blandly and she knew his sister's rudeness had gone unnoticed. Or perhaps he did not see it as rude! Angrily she followed him to the car.

"We shan't be long getting there," he said, letting in the clutch. "It's only a couple of miles."

"What sort of house have they got?"

"About the same size as ours. Different style, though."

Jess sniffed. "Milly got a decorator from London — her and her fancy ideas!"

Stella smiled in the darkness, and a few minutes

later they turned up at a pair of white gates and drew up outside an imposing front door.

The two women were shown to the principal bedroom to take off their coats, and Stella glanced with interest at the muted decor of beige and white.

"Never heard of using such colours," Jess muttered, rubbing the edge of her shoe along the oyster coloured carpet. "This'll be at the cleaners more than it'll be in the room!"

"It's probably nylon," Stella said. "They're easier to keep clean."

"Not my idea of taste. I like something more cheerful."

Stella did not reply and went down to where Matthew was waiting at the door of the lounge. He put his hand under her elbow and propelled her towards a middle-aged woman in the centre of the room.

"Matthew dear, how grand to see you again! And this is Stella." Stella's hand was taken in a friendly clasp and warm brown eyes appraised her. "I'm so pleased to meet Matt's wife at last! His friends have waited a long time for him to marry. Now come and meet Ned."

Milly led them to a bar where a dapper man of about fifty was pouring cocktails. His creased face lit with pleasure as he saw them. "Matt, you old so-and-so! What do you mean by doing us out of a wedding celebration?" He thumped him on the back. "The best of luck to you both. Do I get a kiss from the bride?"

Under Matthew's smiling gaze he kissed Stella heartily on the cheek, then turned to the centre of the room and raised his voice. "Folks, what about a welcome for Matt and his wife?"

He began to sing 'For He's a Jolly Good Fellow' in a cracked falsetto, and gradually all the guests took the refrain until the room rang with singing. In the confusion of noise Stella realized she must look anything but bridal in her plain dress. Indeed, as soon as she had entered the room she had been aware that most of the women looked far more fashionable than she did.

The chorus died away and Matthew bent forward and kissed her full on the mouth. She drew back quickly, and with a fixed smile acknowledged the congratulations that followed, wishing with all her heart that the evening was over instead of beginning.

At dinner she was seated next to her host, with Matthew at the other end of the table, and Ned anxiously watched her pretence of eating.

"What's the matter?" he asked kindly. "You've hardly eaten a thing."

"I'm a bit nervous," she confessed.

"It must be a strain meeting so many people all at once."

"From the way Matthew spoke I thought there would only be a few people here tonight. I never expected a party." She looked at her dress. "I feel out of place wearing this."

"You look fine. But Matt should have warned you. Not that *he'd* think this a big party. He likes people, does Matt — and everyone likes *him*."

"I know." She smiled slightly. "He doesn't realise I'm shy."

The man on the other side of Stella joined in the conversation. "You'll stop better once you make friends. Folk are much warmer here than they are down south."

"I don't think so," she answered. "They seem much more taciturn. It might be the accent of course," she added hastily.

"You mean you don't understand us?"

"Something like that."

He laughed and leaned across the table. "Hey, Matt, how d'you manage to talk to your wife? She's just said she doesn't understand our lingo!"

"We get on all right," Matt replied.

"Some things you don't need a language for!" another man broke in.

Everyone laughed and Stella blushed furiously, conscious of Ned regarding her with sympathy. "Don't mind Bob. He was never one for tact. Our humour's broader here, y'know — but you'll get used to it."

As they left the table Matthew came up and put his arm through hers. "Try not to look so miserable. Aren't you enjoying yourself?"

"I didn't expect so many people."

"I told you it was a dinner-party."

"But not that it was a big one. I'd have worn something different if I'd known."

He looked at her steadily. "You wouldn't have worn that green dress for the smallest party in London. Why did you think it was good enough here?"

"I wasn't able to —" she stopped short and went swiftly ahead of him to the lounge.

Most of the people present were in their late forties and she and Matthew were the youngest couple there until Milly's daughter, a pretty girl of twenty, came in with a crowd of friends. They had been dancing at the golf club and were in high spirits, laughing and joking among themselves. Milly drew the girl aside and introduced her to Stella.

"Welcome to Leeds, Mrs. Armstrong!" Brenda Barrett perched on the arm of her chair. "Sorry I wasn't here to dinner, but I find it such a bore being with older —" She stopped, blushing furiously. "Lord, now I've said the wrong thing! I hope I haven't offended you?"

"Not at all," Stella laughed. "In another ten years I might take that sort of remark personally, but right now, I don't feel much older than you."

"You aren't, are you? I mean you're much younger than Matt."

Stella hid a smile. "He isn't Methusula, you know."

Brenda coloured again. "He always seems older than his age. That's the penalty of success, I suppose. You have the responsibility and worry!" The girl glanced at Matthew who was in the far corner. "He's a darling, though. I had a crush on him for years but it didn't do me any good!" With a flurry of skirts she stood up. "I must be off now. We're going to the music room to dance. Try and pop in later on."

As the evening wore on Stella would have welcomed a chance to accept Brenda's invitation, for Matthew was deep in conversation with a group of men and she was left to talk to the women. The gossip centred on domestic problems, children and grandchildren, and by the time the party broke up she was exhausted with the effort of simulating interest in strangers' lives.

Outside the front door the night air revived her, revived too her irritation with Matthew for leaving her alone the whole evening. The women had been kind enough but she had been conscious of their appraisal, and could imagine them thinking that Matthew had made a fool of himself by marrying someone so stiff and dull.

But Matthew hummed cheerfully all the way home, increasing her irritation to such a degree that she was trembling with nerves as he drove the car into the garage.

Silently she followed Jess into the house, wishing her a brusque goodnight in the hall before going upstairs to her bedroom.

She was taking off her ear-rings when Matthew knocked at the door and came in, untying his tie.

"About that dress you were wearing tonight," he began without preamble. "I owe you an apology."

"For what?"

"For not making arrangements about an allowance for you. You can't buy pretty clothes without money."

Face flaming, she lowered her eyes. "I don't think my appearance has let you down."

93

"I didn't mean that! Your clothes are fine — what there are of them! But you need more. I'll open an account for you in the morning. Will two hundred pounds a month be enough?"

She gasped. "I couldn't . . . it's out of the question."

"For a wife to accept money from her husband? Don't be silly, lass, I can afford it. Now don't let's talk about it any more. It's settled." He came closer. "What did you think of Milly and Ned?"

"They were very nice."

"I knew you'd like 'em. It was a good party, too."

"I didn't enjoy it much." She slipped off her shoes and put on her slippers. "Everyone there was much older than me. Talking about other people's children all evening isn't exactly stimulating."

He grinned. "Wait until you've got a couple of your own."

She sat at the dressing-table and began to comb her hair, but Matthew came up behind her and pulled her back against him.

"When you've a couple o' kids," he repeated, "you'll find plenty to talk about with the other women." His voice was husky. "Stella dearest, I love you so much! Can't you love me a little in return?"

"Oh Matthew, give me time. You promised."

"I know I did. But that party tonight — it seemed a bit of a mockery when they were all congratulating us. Don't let me wait too long, will you, Stella?"

She shook her head dumbly, and with a sigh he kissed her on the cheek and walked out.

A week after the Barrett's dinner-party Brenda rang up and invited her out for tea, calling for her in her own little car and driving with such competence that Stella felt ashamed of her own inability to drive. Once in Leeds they parked the car and wandered round the shops, where Brenda enjoyed herself buying scent and lipstick and gloves.

"You haven't bought a thing!" she exclaimed to Stella.

"I don't need anything."

"Neither do I — but that hasn't stopped me! You're a paragon, if you can come out with me and return home empty-handed!"

Stella laughed but remained adamant. Though Matthew had kept his promise and opened an account for her, she had not touched any of it; to take his money when she was already so emotionally in his debt was out of the question.

She was glad when they left the stores and made their leisurely way to a restaurant for tea, but after a further hour of Brenda's non stop chatter she was heartily glad when the girl suggested they return home.

Her boredom with Brenda made Stella realise how tedious Matthew would find it if she asked him to mix with men and women of *her* age, and that evening, while Jess was out of the dining room, she apologised for finding fault with Milly's party.

"I didn't take any notice of it," he said, as she finished. "If I took account of everything you complained of, we'd have had some mighty rows by now!" She laughed and he looked across at her quickly. "I like that, Stella."

"Like what?"

"The way you laugh. It makes you more human. You should do it more often, sweetheart."

"You must give me reason."

He leaned over the table and caught her hand. "I wish I could. As soon as I've settled things at the factory we'll go away. Perhaps by then we'll be — happier."

"I hope so."

He patted her hand and then let it go.

"Matthew," she said suddenly, "why must you always call me sweetheart and lass?"

His look was quizzical. "I was wondering when you

95

were going to ask me that."

"I'm sorry. I didn't mean to —"

"No need to apologise. But I'll make a bargain with you. You stop saying 'frightfully', 'ghastly' and 'really' and I won't say sweetheart and lass!"

"Touché!" She pulled a face. "I asked for that!"

He repeated her smile, though his eyes remained serious as he said: "Does my accent bother you? Be honest with me, Stella."

"I notice it," she said carefully.

"But does it bother you?" he persisted.

She bit her lip. Had he posed this question when they were in London, she would unhesitatingly have said yes, but in the last few months she had grown accustomed to it, and found it warming and friendly — except when spoken by her sister-in-law!

"It doesn't bother me at all," she said firmly. "Think how dull it would be if we all spoke the same way."

With a pleased grunt he resumed his meal, and anything she might have added was forestalled by Jess' return.

After dinner they went into the drawing-room and Jess settled herself on the settee with her knitting while Matthew sat back in an armchair and filled his pipe.

"What about giving us a tune, lass?" he said suddenly. "You've not played for a long time."

Glad of something to do, she stood up and went to the piano, starting with *Clair de Lune* and *Greensleeves*, before going into the *Moonlight Sonata*. As the last note died away, Jess yawned prodigiously.

"You play quite well, but I can't say I like your taste. Why don't you give us something with more of a tune? That lot fair sent me to sleep."

"You needn't have stayed to listen," Stella said icily.

"Don't be offended with Jess," Matthew said hastily. "She's never been very musical."

"I don't care whether she is, or isn't. But that's no reason for her to deprecate what other people enjoy."

Jess stood up with a flounce of skirts. "If you've quite finished talking about me . . ."

The door banged behind her, and Stella lifted her hands in a hopeless gesture, expecting Matthew to make some comment. When he did, she was disagreeably surprised.

"You'd no reason to upset Jess like that. You're too quick to take offence with her."

"I was playing for *you* — music *you* like."

"But Jess was here too. You should have remembered that."

Too hurt to defend herself further — not that she thought defence was needed, Stella lapsed into silence, excusing herself several moments later to retire to her room.

Matthew's championship of his sister rankled bitterly with Stella, increasing the chasm that separated her from him. How could he expect her to feel close to him when he always sided against her in an argument? When he refused to let her have any say in the running of his home? What a mockery it made of his promise that she would be able to do as she liked once she was his wife! Grey Walls was far more Jess's home than anyone else's. And Matthew liked it that way! It was this knowledge which rankled more than anything. Night after night he came home to the same stodgy meals of hotpot or stew; of potatoes and cabbage and a sherry trifle that could easily have passed for a bread pudding with shop bought custard passed over it! And it wasn't as though Matthew didn't appreciate well cooked meals. In London he had always chosen the menu with imagination and understanding. But here, in his own home, he was frightened to come to terms with his sister.

As if knowing Stella's feelings, Jess went out of

her way to be condescending, and though there were many times when a row could have developed, Stella resolutely refused to play into her sister-in-law's hands. If anything she made a greater effort to be friendly, even though the overtures met with continual rebuffs. When Stella made conversation, Jess complained of idle people with idle tongues, and if she was silent would remark that she had not expected her brother to marry someone who could not be bothered to speak to ordinary folk. She sniffed audibly when Stella wore one of her trousseau dresses, and having grown accustomed to her mother's criticism of her simple clothes, Stella was surprised by her sister-in-law's envy. But her offer to go shopping with Jess was met with an affronted refusal, and she passed no comment on the new tweeds and fussy dresses that made their appearance, though she could not help thinking that for someone who professed to despise fashion, Jess was displaying an extravagance out of keeping with her economy in running her brother's household.

Mrs. Percy wrote regularly each week, and Stella wondered what her mother would say if she knew the position that existed between herself and Matthew.

"When are you coming to London?" (one letter began). "I'm lonely now that you're away and Adrian's at the Academy all day. He's settling down well, and I'm trying to make sure he doesn't get mixed up with those awful young men again. There's so much I want to ask you, Stella — can't you come down for a few days? It must be depressing to be stuck in the wilds. The winter's grim in London, but it must be worse where you are, and a change would do you good."

With this part of the letter Stella heartily agreed. Many times she longed for the theatres, concerts and friends she had once taken for granted. Although its position had much to commend it, Grey Walls was a long way from town, and a visit to Leeds entailed a long, tedious bus journey. Once or twice she had telephoned for a taxi, but Jess had been so scathing in her comments that eventually she had stopped doing it. She had always imagined she would have a car of her own to drive, but to her surprise Matthew only had one, which he himself took to the factory each day.

"Never could stand being driven," he apologised, "or else I'd have had a chauffeur. But I'll see about getting a run-about for you."

"That would be ideal," she enthused. "I'd like to get out more."

"Take a taxi, sweetheart."

"You can't always get one," she lied. "And anyway," she added truthfully, "you can never get one to bring you home again if it's after four o'clock. The rush hour here, is worse than London."

"Then come home earlier. You've got all day to do your bits and pieces!"

With an effort she controlled herself. "If you go to a matinèe or concert, you can't dictate the time they end!"

"You've a point there," he conceded. "A sports car is the answer."

"I don't mind what you buy. A second hand car would —"

"There's no need for that," he interrupted. "I can afford to buy you the best!"

He held out his hand and, as she took it, Jess came in, her hard brown eyes raking them.

"Don't mind me," she said with false heartiness. "It's good to see you acting like lovebirds."

Matthew chuckled but Stella dropped his hand and moved away from him.

"Don't tell me I've embarrassed you, Stella?" Jess grinned. "I never thought you'd still be shy with Matt."

"I'm not shy with Matthew," Stella said coolly, "only with *you!*"

99

No more mention was made of the car, but with every passing day Stella anticipated finding one waiting for her in the drive. During their brief engagement Matthew had been generous in the giving of presents, and had lavished gifts not only on herself but on Adrian and her mother too. But the sympathetic man she had known in London was nothing like the pre-occupied tycoon he had now become, and though she realised he was still absorbed with final settlement of the strike, she resented his obtuseness in doing nothing to alleviate her loneliness.

Pride refused to let her remind him of his promise, and as the days passed, anticipation gave way to hurt and then to anger. Why had she married a man about whom she knew so little? Why hadn't she at least had the sense to visit his home first? Sight of Jess alone would have been sufficient warning of what she was letting herself in for!

Yet there was a lot about Matthew that she liked, and when she was not smarting under his indifference to her problems, she was conscious of vague stirrings of affection which could — she felt — have blossomed into something deeper if they had been given a chance to be on their own.

At the end of March Stella received a letter from Charles telling her he was coming to Leeds on business and would like to see her. The brief note gave her surprising pleasure, and she replied immediately, inviting him to dinner. How wonderful to talk to someone who spoke her language and understood her point of view!

She mentioned his coming to Jess who shrugged indifferently. "I'll be out most of Friday. You should have given me warning."

"I didn't know until today. But I can do the dinner myself."

"Not in my kitchen, you won't. You can't have two women running the same house. I'll prepare something for you to heat up. Which would you prefer — hotpot or steak and kidney pie?"

"Do you think we could have veal escappoles?" Stella said carefully. "They only need frying and I could —"

"Veal's too dear," Jess retorted. "I'll do the steak and kidney with some extra potatoes and cabbage and sherry trifle to finish with."

"Couldn't we have something other than cabbage?"

"I'll try for sprouts. But I don't think your fancy friend will object to a good, wholesome meal."

She stalked out and Stella furiously paced the room. Her position here was intolerable. She was nothing more than a stranger in a home that was supposed to be her own. Matthew would have to do something. She could not go on this way any longer.

"I was afraid this would happen," he said when she tackled him about it later that evening, choosing a moment when Jess was in the kitchen. "Two women can never share the same kitchen without quarrelling!"

"We're *not* sharing the same kitchen," Stella commented. "I'm not even allowed in it!"

"That's something most women wouldn't complain of! Why do you want to bother with the domestic side if Jess is willing —"

"Because this is supposed to be *my* home and I'd like some say in the way it's run. You promised you'd talk to Jess about it, but you haven't said a word."

"I want to do it in my own way," he said quickly, and was about to continue when Jess's heavy tread was heard in the hall. Clamping his mouth around his pipe, he lapsed into silence.

Moodily Stella picked up a book and began to read. But it was difficult to concentrate on fiction when reality kept impinging on her thoughts, and after a while she flung the book aside and went to her room.

She was still at the dressing-table brushing her hair when there was a knock at the door, and knowing it was Matthew she could not stop herself trembling, though her voice as she bade him come in, was cool and self-possessed.

"You're annoyed with me," he said without hedging. "I just want you to know I haven't forgotten I said I'd talk to Jess. But she's looked after my home for years and I don't want her to think I'm trying to get rid of her now I don't need her."

"No one's trying to get rid of her."

"*We* know that — but she doesn't. The minute I say anything to her, that's what she'll think."

"Then you'll never be able to tell her!"

"I will. I promise you that." His eyes were pleading. "Give me time, Stella."

His words reminded her of her own pleas to him the day after their marriage, and her scathing reply died before it was uttered. No matter how angry he made her, the memory of her wedding night prevented her making any demands on him. All she could do was request. Only when she was his wife in the full sense of the word would she have the right to expect him to put her wishes before those of another woman. Yet how could she learn to respond to him when Jess was a continual barrier between them? When his defence of his ill-mannered sister destroyed any warmth she might have felt for him?

Unaware of her thoughts he strode over and pulled her to her feet, and for the first time she realised she was wearing nothing beneath the fine silk of her negligee. She tried to move away from him but the action inflamed the passion he was trying to hold in check, and he held her more tightly and buried his lips in the soft tangle of hair at the nape of her neck.

"How much longer?" he whispered. "I want you so much. — You're beautiful, Stella, so beautiful."

Lifting his head, he found her lips, his hands caressing the smooth skin on her shoulders and moving down to cup the gently swelling curve of her breasts.

Unable to stop herself Stella responded to his touch, twining her hands around his neck and stroking his hair.

"Sweetheart," he said eagerly, and pulled her closer still, his heart thudding so heavily that she could feel it against her own. "I want you, Stella. I want you. Don't let Jess come between us."

The name acted on her like an electric shock. Gagging nausea threatened to overwhelm her and the desire she had felt for him vanished. What a fool he was to have mentioned his sister's name. What a blind insensitive fool! Hating herself for having been aroused, she hated him the more for having aroused her, and unable to hide her look of revulsion, she turned back to the dressing-table and blindly handed him a tissue.

"You've got lipstick all over you, Matthew."

He wiped it off, never taking his eyes from her. "What's the matter, Stella? A minute ago you —"

"I'm tired," she interrupted. "I want to be left alone."

The warmth left his face, leaving it bleak and sad. "I understand. I'm sorry."

He was at the door when she spoke his name again, turning with such eagerness that she was furious with herself for being so stupid. Why couldn't she at least have waited till the morning before making her request. But it was too late now. "I just wanted to know if I can borrow the car in the morning," she said hurriedly.

"Of course." He spoke with an effort. "I'll get Bob to drive you. Do you have much to do?"

"I want to get some vegetables and some nuts and chocolates. Charles has a sweet tooth."

"You must be looking forward to seeing him."

"I am." She spoke without expression. "He's a good friend of mine."

"*I* couldn't come and see you so calmly if I'd lost

103

you to another man," Matthew said bluntly. "I'd want to sock him on the jaw!"

She could not help laughing. "You needn't worry about Charles. He isn't the fighting type!"

"I wouldn't worry even if he were."

Stella knew he was speaking the truth, and looking at his broad shoulders and strong, clenched hands, she could not avoid a momentary feeling of power.

"Try and get home early tomorrow," she said huskily. "I'd like you here when Charles arrives."

"I'll leave sharp at five. Goodnight, lass. And remember . . . I love you."

When Stella went downstairs the following morning the car was already in the drive with Bob at the wheel, and her sister-in-law was in the kitchen with her hands deep in flour, her sallow face flushed from the heat of the oven.

"I'm going out, Jess. Is there anything I can get you?"

"No, thanks. I've got everything in."

"I thought your order wouldn't be delivered until some time this morning. That's why I'm going to town — I want to get something special."

"I thought we'd decided on the food."

Stella moistened lips that were suddenly dry. "I thought we'd have something more exciting than mashed potatoes and cabbage."

Jess flung down her wooden spoon. "Then you'd better cook the dinner yourself! I've tried to do my best for you ever since you arrived, but you're too much the lady for me. I've had enough of your complaints. I'll not be your skivvy any longer!"

"You're anything but my skivvy! This is as much your home as mine, but I'm your brother's wife and the mistress of his house."

"Bit of a change for you to be mistress of anything! Looks as if it's gone to your head! Well, I'll

104

not have you throwing your weight about while I'm here!"

"Then perhaps it would be better if you left." The words were out before Stella could stop them, but once they were said she grew reckless. "If you feel you're working like a skivvy, the best thing is for you to find a home of your own."

"We'll see what Matt has to say about that! You'll be laughing the other side of your face when I've told him." Jess untied her apron and threw it on the floor. "Pick it up and get to work. You talk so fine, let's see what you can do for a change!"

The kitchen door banged behind her and Stella sat down on a chair and buried her head in her hands.

"Why, Mrs. Matthew, whatever's the matter?"

She straightened to see Elsie looking at her in concern. "I suppose you've had words with Miss Jess. But don't fret, she'll come round."

"Not in time to prepare the dinner," Stella said ruefully. "I'm not a bad cook myself, but I don't fancy having a visitor to dinner the first time I cook in a strange kitchen." She stood up. "We'd better dine out."

"So that's why you had a fight?" Elsie grinned. "I bet it was the cabbage and mash! I knew you wouldn't like it."

"But I do," Stella said quickly. "Cabbage is very tasty and —"

"Not when you've got guests," Elsie ploughed on, ignoring the defence. "My mother was cook at one of the big houses on the other side of the moors, so I know just what you ought to have. And I can do it, too."

Stella looked at her with dawning hope. "Are you trying to tell me you can cook?"

"Yes. I'm not as good as Mum, but I know what's what."

"Why didn't you tell me before?"

105

"You never asked me, and anyway Miss Jess has always done the cooking."

"I'm glad you've told me. If you like cooking and you're good at it, there's no reason why you can't do it if Mr. Armstrong agrees."

"Will you let me do the dinner tonight as a trial?"

"By all means. We can have grilled grapefruit to begin with — that's easy — and I know the trifle's been made, so you —"

"There's no cause to be having grapefruit," Elsie interrupted, "nor trifle. We can eat that up tomorrow." Rummaging in a drawer she took out a pencil and pad. "If I write out what I need, perhaps you could get it for me."

"I'll get whatever you want," Stella said happily. "Just name it!"

As if her quarrel with Jess had given a fillip to her otherwise easy acceptance of Matthew's position, Stella spent money as if she really was Mrs. Matthew Armstrong, and for the first time since her marriage bought all the delicacies she had not seen since she had left London.

It was nearly one o'clock when she returned home and, entering the kitchen, found Elsie — unfamiliar in a long white apron — humming cheerfully as she rolled pastry.

"This is for the mushrooms, ma'am," she greeted Stella like a fellow conspirator. "I thought we'd have mushroom boats as hors d'oeuvres, then asparagus as a vegetable on a separate dish."

"What a good idea!" Stella untied the packages. "I bought a tin of *foie gras* for the hors d'oeuvres, but as you've made mushroom boats we'll have it tomorrow instead. Do you know if Mr. Armstrong likes it?"

"I shouldn't think he's had the chance. Miss Jess would never buy anything as pricey as that!"

"Has my sister-in-law gone out yet?"

"She's in her room, changing. Gave me a look fit

106

to kill when she saw me dolled up like this, but never a word. Now then, Mrs. Matthew, you go and do the flowers and leave everything else to me."

For the next few hours Stella busied herself with the mass of flowers she had bought. The bright daffodils relieved the heavy gloom of the hall, and the mahogany dining-table looked resplendent with tulips reflected in its polished surface.

Before she went to change she set the table with the ornate silver cutlery and crystal glasses. The flowered china dinner service bespoke Jess's taste, but the damask cloth fell in sleek folds almost to the floor, giving the room an elegance it had never had before.

She was in the bathroom when Matthew's car crunched on the gravel drive and she was pleased he had made the effort to get back before Charles arrived. Hurriedly she went into her bedroom and put on a grey chiffon dress almost the same colour as her eyes, fastening the long sleeves with tiny, multi-coloured buttons that matched the wide jewelled belt at her waist. She applied her make-up more lavishly than usual, disguising the paleness of her cheeks with rouge and darkening her lashes heavily with mascara.

She hesitated outside Matthew's dressing-room, wondering if he would be ready in time. But her marriage had taught her that he was a slow and careful dresser, and with a faint smile she went on her way downstairs.

The front door slammed resoundingly as she turned the corner of the corridor and she realised Jess had left the house without seeing her. Heaven only knew what tales the woman would bear to her friends! For the moment it did not seem important, and she went into the drawing-room and stirred the fire before going to the cocktail cabinet to set out the sherry glasses, irrationally nervous at the thought of seeing Charles again. What would his attitude to her be and how

107

would he react to Matthew? He had a discerning eye and would be quick to notice the relationship between them was not all it should be.

The door opened and Matthew came in, his face ruddy from it's usual brisk wash with cold water.

"I'm glad you were able to get home early, Matthew."

"I told you I would. It's only right I should be here the first time you have a guest." He appraised her. "You're looking very nice. If I'd known you were going to wear a dinner-dress I'd have changed as well. Still, I don't suppose Charles will have bothered to bring his dinner-jacket just for one night, so I'll be keeping him company."

She touched his arm impulsively before she looked at her watch. "I hope he won't be late or dinner will be spoilt. It's the first time I've given one and I want it to go off well."

Matthew stood in front of the fire and clasped his hands behind his back. "I suppose it was being anxious that made you act hasty towards Jess. The poor girl was most upset."

"How do you know?"

"I saw her when I came in. She was on her way out and burst into tears when she saw me."

"Jess crying?"

"Yes, crying. She's a woman, you know, and has feelings just like you. I daresay she said a few things she shouldn't have, but she's very upset."

"If anyone has a right to be upset it's me, not your sister," Stella said indignantly. "Surely I'm entitled to choose what I want for dinner without her taking it as an insult."

"It was your manner she didn't like," persisted Matthew.

"I didn't like hers either! She isn't the same person in front of you as she is when we're alone together."

"You're imagining things. Jess is too simple to play a double game."

"If Jess is simple, heaven preserve me from someone complex! All I did was suggest we had another vegetable instead of cabbage and mash, and she threw a tantrum like the Queen of Sheba!"

"Because you were rude to her."

"Rude?" Stella's voice rose. "What about her rudeness to me? I don't come running to you every time your sister and I have a row, but there have been plenty of times when I could."

"I respect you for keeping quiet about it."

"You wouldn't defend me even if you knew!"

He was silenced, but only momentarily, and when he continued it was to ignore her comment. "If Jess is edgy with you, you'll have to make allowances for her. You're more intelligent and it won't be as hard for you."

"Why must I bother?" she cried angrily. "Why can't Jess have a home of her own?"

"What difference does it make if she's here? She's hardly playing gooseberry to a couple of lovebirds!"

"That's not the point." For the first time Stella refused to be sidetracked. "Even if I wanted to be alone with you, I never get the chance. Yet you don't even care!"

"Of course I care! You should know that without my having to say so. But this is Jess's home. I can't tell her to go."

"Not even for me?" Stella asked softly. "Not even if you knew we'd have more chance of being happy together if we were on our own?"

His eyes were anguished. "Jess has kept house for me for ten years. I can't tell her to go now."

Unable to believe she had lost, Stella went to stand by the window, staring out into a darkness no darker than her thoughts. When it came to the final choice between his sister and his wife, Matthew had shown where his loyalty lay. It was a decision she had never anticipated, so sure had she been that when it came to the final choice he would choose her. Now she knew exactly what his feelings for her were; not the warm, cherishing love she had foolishly expected, but a venal desire.

"Forgive me, lass," he whispered behind her. "Try and see it from my point of view."

"A car's coming into the drive," she said, ignoring his remark. "It's Charles. I'll open the door. Elsie's busy in the kitchen."

"I'll go," he offered, but she brushed past him and opened the front door to find Charles on the step.

"Charles, darling!"

"Stella, my dear." He kissed her cheek. "It's good to see you again. Nearly three months."

He stepped into the hall and took off his coat. In his dinner-jacket he looked as immaculate as ever, the soft white shirt without a wrinkle, the black tie perfectly placed.

Matthew came forward to greet him. "How are you, Heyward? Come and warm yourself by the fire. If the flames reach the mantelpiece, you'll know you're in Yorkshire. Now what about a drink? Whisky, gin, cherry brandy?"

"No one has cherry brandy *before* dinner?" Stella put in. "Charles will have sherry — unless you've changed your tastes since we last met?"

"You know me better than that." Charles nodded to Matthew. "Sherry, please."

The big hands were unsteady on the decanter. "Will you have the same, Stella?"

"Please."

Matthew filled the glasses and Charles took his and raised it to them. "Your very good health — and happiness."

"Thanks." Matthew smiled at Stella. "To our happiness."

Her lips curved in a smile, but her eyes were bleak and she turned immediately to Charles. "Have you seen Mother lately?"

"I dined with her last night. There was a concert at the Academy and I took her to hear Adrian play. I must say he was extremely good. I think he'll go a long way."

Her eyes shone. "I hope so! It means a lot to him."

"And to you too."

'I hope he justifies your faith," Matthew put in. "I wouldn't mind having a well-known brother-in-law. Quite a feather in my cap."

"I wasn't looking at it from that point of view," she said quietly. "Now if you'll excuse me I'll see how Elsie's getting on."

Elsie had prepared the meal expertly and Stella felt it triumphantly proved her point that Jess was not indispensable. The girl had changed into uniform and served each course as if she had nothing to do with it's preparation, her face only occasionally betraying her as Matthew or Charles gave a murmur of appreciation.

"By heavens, that was good!" Matthew beamed as he finished his sweet. "Well Charles, no one can say we can't cook up here. Yorkshire food's still the best."

"Cote de veau is hardly a Yorkshire dish," Stella said crushingly.

"But a Yorkshire lass cooked it!"

"I'm surprised you want to remember who cooked it!"

Matthew grinned at Charles. "My sister usually takes care of the food, but Stella likes fancier dishes so she and Jess parted company for the evening."

Furious that he had misinterpreted the facts in this way, she gave an exclamation of anger. If Matthew could not be truthful, he could at least have been loyal!

"Matthew's being ingenuous," she said deliberately.

"The truth is that Jess and I had a frightful row this morning."

Charles looked at his host and composed his expression into one of diplomatic commiseration. "You must find it a tricky situation."

"Not at all," Stella said before Matthew could reply. "My loving husband sides with his sister!"

Matthew pushed back his chair, only the pulse at the side of his temple indicating his mood. "Let's have coffee in the other room. It's hot in here."

Not waiting to see if they would follow him, he strode out, and he was pouring the brandy when Stella and Charles came into the drawing-room. While they sipped it they talked about people he did not know, and unable to join in the conversation he let his mind wander, brooding over the argument he had had with Stella earlier that evening.

Did she really believe he did not want to be alone with her? Was she so innocent that she did not know how impossible it would have been for him to have sat alone with her night after night without making love to her? Had it not been for Jess' presence, nothing could have stopped him from flinging himself into Stella's arms and begging her to love him. And what a fool she would think him if he did! Only by remaining aloof did he have any chance of winning her. One false step, one glimpse of his overwhelming need of her, and she might easily take flight. But how hard it was not to touch her when he ached to hold her body in his arms. So soft and fragile. Not like her sharp tongue!

He sighed heavily. Surely she had enough sense to understand his attitude towards Jess? You couldn't ask somebody to leave when they were all the family you had . . . Yet Stella was his family too . . . or nearly. If only she could let herself go; lose the fear that was preventing her from admitting she loved him. And she did love him: he was certain of it. It was apparent in the way she returned his kisses, in her swift response to his touch.

"You must think us very rude talking about people you don't know."

Charles's voice broke in on his thoughts and Matthew looked at them with a smile. "Don't mind me. I knew you and Stella would like a natter. It's a long time since she's seen one of her own kind."

"There's no need to talk as if you're a foreigner!" Stella cried.

"Sometimes I feel like one!"

"I know what you mean," Charles put in tactfully. "I'd probably feel the same if I married a Yorkshire girl."

"I can't imagine you at a loss with anyone," Stella smiled. "You'd be at home with the Eskimos!"

Embarrassed, Charles looked at his glass. "Would you care to play for me?" he asked. "It's a long while since I heard you."

"What would you like?"

"Can't you guess —?"

"The Chopin *Nocturne's* been your favourite for so long I thought you'd be tired of it by now!"

Her fingers ran over the keys and, watching her, Matthew wondered what she would say if she knew that at eighteen he had walked five miles to hear his first concert? The subsequent years of hard work had left him little time to indulge his secret liking, and it wounded him deeply that Stella, who could have helped him so much, had not been willing to help him at all. It was weeks since she had played for him, and then it had only been on sufferance, for the moment Jess had come into the room she had used it as an excuse to stop. The soft notes died away and he cleared his throat. "That was grand, lass."

She ignored him. "Did you like it, Charles?"

"Need you ask? You're playing better than ever."

113

Charles turned to Matthew. "I envy you being able to hear her when you like."

"I don't — she never plays for me these days."

Charles looked at Stella in surprise and she shrugged at his unspoken question. "I don't like playing when people are bored. My sister-in-law doesn't like music."

"She's not here, now," Matthew put in eagerly.

Stella trembled with anger. If Jess had been here he would have been afraid to ask her to play in case it precipitated a quarrel. Why should his sister's disapproval mean so much to him when her own meant so little?

"Come on, lass, play anything you think suits me."

There was a pause, then she threw back her head and her hands crashed down on the keys in a resounding cacophony of chords. She strummed with such vulgar embellishments that it was several minutes before Matthew recognized it as an ugly parody of a Yorkshire miner's song; but he listened without a flicker of emotion until, with a last strident trill, she finished and swung round to look at him.

"Well," she demanded, "did you like it?"

"Very much." Beads of perspiration shone on his forehead, but his voice was quiet. "Quite a rousing version of the old song."

Charles stood up awkwardly. "I really must be going. It's late."

With an effort Matthew extended his hand. "It was nice seeing you. I hope you'll come again when you're this way."

"Thank you. Will you see me to the door, Stella?"

In the hall Charles caught her hand. "Good-bye, my dear. I'll phone your mother and tell her how I found you." His grip tightened. "Watch your step, Stella, you were unnecessarily cruel."

"Not without reason!" She pulled her hand away.

"Give my love to Mother and tell her I'll be down to see her soon."

She closed the door and went back to the drawing-room. Charles had no right to pass judgement when he did not know the circumstances. Without a word she crossed to the piano and shut the lid, then turned out the standard lamp and prepared to leave the room.

"Don't go yet," Matthew said. "I want to talk to you."

"Can't it wait till morning?"

"No," he said tightly, "it can't. How dare you insult me like that in front of Charles?"

"Because of what I played?"

"It was the *way* you played it."

"Really Matthew, you're exaggerating. I only —"

"Insult my manners and my tastes," he roared, "but don't insult my intelligence!" He flung his cigar into the fire. "I am as I am, and there's nothing I can do about it. I told you months ago that neither of us would change, and I meant it! I won't put up with your behaviour any longer."

"And I won't put up with yours! How can you defend your horrible sister against *me* . . ." she choked on the words and turned away from him.

"Leave Jess out of it," he said. "Most couples have family trouble, but *ours* goes deeper than that."

"You can't separate the two. If Jess weren't here, we wouldn't still be strangers to each other."

"You can't blame Jess for our wedding night! You didn't want me then and you don't want me now. If you're so keen on honesty why aren't you honest with yourself? You're ashamed of me, that's what you are! Ashamed because I don't talk and act like your fine friend Charles! It wasn't too much trouble to get all dressed up for *him*, was it? Nor to make a special dinner that —"

"I change for dinner every night," she said hotly, "and I'd order food for *you* if your sister would let

115

me! But the first time I say anything to her she acts like the Mad Woman of Chailot!"

"Because you wanted to throw her out of her own home!"

"Her home!" Stella cried. "Her home and your home, but never mine!"

"What right do you have to call it yours when you're not my wife — when you still look at me with hate? You didn't turn me away that first night because I was a stranger to you, but because you despised me. Because you felt superior!"

"That's not true!" she cried. "I was afraid of you — and I still am. I've tried to get closer to you — heaven knows I've tried — but what chance have I had with Jess snooping around the whole time. We haven't been alone three times in as many months."

"Did you never wonder why?" he shouted. "Do you think I can *bear* to be alone with you night after night, knowing that if I wanted to I could make you surrender? Don't shake your head like that. I've made love to enough women to know I could have had you if I'd wanted you that way — and made you enjoy it too!" His voice sank lower. "But I respected you too much. I thought you too far above me. Stella — my star, I used to call you, a sleeping beauty who'd wake up for me! Well, for all I care you can stay asleep for ever! If *you* don't want me, there's plenty who do!"

Throwing a chair out of his path he lunged violently from the room, the glasses on the sideboard tinkling as the front door slammed.

The house was quiet without Matthew's voice ringing in her ears, but it was a quiet that held no peace, and shivering she huddled close to the fire. The evening had been damned from the moment he had refused to tell Jess to find a home of her own. Hurt by his lack of loyalty she had made no effort to hide her anger from Charles, and stupidly Matthew had tried

116

to gloss over the reason for it, endeavouring to make her bitter quarrel with Jess seem like a childish argument that would disappear by morning.

Yet knowing he had been at fault did not mitigate her own cruelty to him, nor blind her to the fact that he was right when he accused her of having married him without love. Tears poured down her cheeks but she did not know for whom she was crying — for herself or Matthew or them both. How badly she had behaved to him; her affection so weak that the liking she had felt for him when she was alone, had always been destroyed by his presence; the need he roused in her always swamped by her condescension. She had been wrong to wait until her love for him could equal the desire she felt. Love would come if she surrendered to his passion instead of imposing so many conditions. As if a blue-blooded background was better than a self-made man with courage and determination to succeed — as if polished manners and a perfect accent were more important than warmth and sincerity. How could she have tried to destroy Matthew's belief in himself when his only folly had been to love her? What right did she have to change him when he was already so much better than she deserved?

Racked by remorse, she longed to talk to him, to tell him she had been wrong. Yet she knew that words alone would not be apology enough. Only action — loving action — could set their marriage on the right course.

But what of Jess? Could she and Matthew be happy while his sister lived with them? Somehow she doubted it. But perhaps when she had shown Matthew that she could care for him, his loyalty would be given to her instead. It seemed a logical thing to assume, and she was angry with herself for not having realised this before.

Anxiously she waited for him to come home, but at two o'clock she was still sitting in front of the burnt-out fire, and only when the room became cold did she go to bed, undressing with shaking fingers and shivering uncontrollably as she slipped between the sheets. She lay for a long time listening for the sound of Matthew's car, longing for the warmth of his arms and the comfort of his forgiveness, but the silence remained unbroken, and at last she drifted into an uneasy sleep.

CHAPTER NINE

STELLA was roused by the creaking of the stairs and switched on the lamp to look at her watch. Half past five! Without pause to think, she threw aside the bedclothes and ran into the dressing-room.

Matthew was by the wardrobe, but he did not turn and she moved towards him hesitantly.

"Matthew," she whispered, "I don't know what to say! Every time I come into this room I seem to apologize."

"It's too late for that now." He sat down to unlace his shoes, and with a little cry she knelt at his side.

"Don't say it's too late! I behaved like a beast and I deserved everything you said. But if you'll give me another chance, I'll do anything, anything!"

"It's too late," he reiterated.

"It's never too late to apologize! Oh Matthew, say you forgive me." She clasped his knees. "Hold me and say you forgive me."

"I can't." He looked at her without expression. "If you had spoken like this a few hours ago, I might have done. But not now. I can't come to you from the arms of another woman — even if it was you who drove me there!"

For a split second Stella was not sure she had heard correctly. Then the anguish on his face communicated itself to her and, stunned, she stood up and backed away from him. "Are you . . . are you serious?"

"Even men like me don't joke about things like that."

Still she went on staring at him, seeing him recede further and further into the distance until his face became a pale blur.

"Stella!" His voice was faint and far away. "Are you all right? Come and sit down."

"Keep away from me!" She put out a hand to ward him off. "Don't touch me."

Gathering her strength she stumbled from the room, closing the door on all her hopes for their future.

In the remaining hours till daybreak she paced her room. Never had she thought that Matthew could have acted this way. What value did his love for her have now? What trust could she ever place on his feelings? She was too distraught to analyse how much of her reaction to his confession was hurt pride and how much genuine disgust; she only knew she never wanted to see him again.

Slowly she dressed, making up her face automatically before she went downstairs to find Elsie laying the drawing-room fire, familiar again in her blue-and-white check dress.

"Why Mrs. Matthew, you're up early!"

"I'm going to London."

"I'll fix your breakfast."

"Just coffee please."

Elsie regarded her curiously. "Do you feel all right? You look ever so pale."

"I'm fine thanks. Just tired."

With a forced smile Stella returned to her room and started to pack. By the time Elsie came up with her coffee she had nearly finished, and sat down to drink it.

She was sipping her second cup when the dressing-room door opened, and though she did not look round she was acutely aware of Matthew looking at her.

"So you're going?" he said harshly.

"What did you expect me to do?"

"Just what you are doing — running away." His step came closer. "Look at me, Stella."

Reluctantly she turned, aware that he was paler and more grim than she had ever seen him.

"I'm not going to make any excuses for last night," he said. "I'll regret it all my life. But you can't turn

120

back the clock, and I've got to go on from where I left off."

"That's why I'm leaving — when you're alone, you'll be able to go on more conveniently!"

"I suppose it's too much to expect you to admit your share of the blame?"

She shrugged. "I was partly responsible. But if you love someone, you don't run to another woman the first time you have a quarrel."

"The first time you quarrel," he echoed. "That's a joke! You'll be telling me next we lived in loving harmony until last night."

"You don't know what love means." Bitterness made her search for the cruellest thing she could say. "You're like an animal — and just as easily satisfied!"

He lunged forward and she shrank back, afraid he was going to hit her. But with an effort that made the muscles of his jaw bulge, he drew away again. "I don't intend to defend myself. You wouldn't understand if I did. You don't *want* to. But we have to face facts."

"I already have. That's why I'm leaving you."

"You're not going anywhere till you've heard me out. From the minute I married you I've treated your family as if they were my own, and now —"

"You want your pound of flesh!"

"I want you to stay here a few months longer," he concluded. "I don't fancy being made a laughing-stock by having you run off three months after we're married."

"You should have thought of that before you . . ." She clenched her hands. "I suppose you'll stop Adrian's allowance if I do? That's just the vulgar sort of bargaining I should have expected from you!"

"Whether you go or stay won't affect my arrangements for your brother," he said harshly. "I was hoping you'd do it as a favour to me. I know it isn't done among your fine friends to remind a woman of a debt, but as you've always pointed out, I'm no gentle-man!"

The dressing-room door banged behind him and she sank on the bed and rested her head in her hands. If only Matthew's behaviour last night *could* cancel her debt to him. But unfortunately it didn't. For the next two years at least, Adrian would be financially dependent on him, and though she hated the thought of having to remain here, she knew she could not refuse Matthew's request to do so.

Without giving herself time to think she called his name, and he walked in, tucking his handkerchief into the pocket of his suit.

"Well?"

"I'll do as you ask," she said quickly. "I can't repay the money you've spent on Adrian, and if staying here a few more months will even things up between us . . ." She shrugged and, turning her back on him, met his eyes through the mirror. "I need hardly say that our marriage is finished. I'll put on an act in front of your friends, but you might as well know that as long as I live, I shall despise you."

His jaw clenched. "Cruel tongues have driven many men into other women's arms."

"I'm not interested how people like you find your compensation. I'm glad for your sake you're so easily satisfied!"

She averted her face, and when she next looked up he had gone.

Not until she went into the dining-room for lunch, did Stella see her sister-in-law.

"You're looking washed out," Jess commented, handing her a plate of soup. "Must have been the strain of your dinner party!"

Stella refused to be drawn into an argument, and Jess said no more until she was stacking the dishes.

"Well, did Matthew say you were right?"

"About what?"

"About wanting me to leave here."

"We didn't discuss it. Charles arrived soon after Matthew came home, and by the time he left I was too tired to bother."

"Changed your tune, haven't you? I was expecting you to tell me to pack my bags and go."

Her obvious triumph was too much for Stella. "As far as I'm concerned you can stay here forever!"

Scraping back her chair, she ran out of the room, leaving Jess staring after her in astonishment.

During the following week Stella saw little of Matthew, and neither knew nor cared whether Jess realised something was wrong. The woman would know soon enough that her victory was complete: in a few months she would have her brother to herself.

Spring came in with a rush and almost overnight the buds on the trees flared open. As the weather grew warmer, Stella went for long, lonely walks, often not returning for lunch or tea. Music was her only other consolation. It soothed her and gave her a satisfaction that even Adrian did not seem to find in it, for where she could play solely for pleasure, his compulsion was a rigorous task-master that would not let him alone. Indeed, in his rare letters to her there was an under-current of restlessness that was faintly disquieting, almost as if he resented this gift that stopped him enjoying the indolent life he would have liked to lead.

It was not until one morning in the middle of April that, reading an unexpected letter from him, her fears materialised.

"Dear Sis," (he began, in his usual scrawling hand), "I haven't written for a while because I've been busy preparing for the end of term concert. I'm taking part in a big way and hope you'll come for it. Try and bring Matthew too — he might as well see how his investment is getting on! Which brings me to the fact that *my* investments are lousy. I needed some extra cash and took a chance on the 'gee-gees'. Unfortunately the one I backed ran as if it had three legs, so I'm worse off than before. I've got to find a couple of hundred pounds and you're the only person I can ask. I'm sure Matthew's very generous to you, and hope you'll be the same to me! For heaven's sake don't ask him, though. I'm counting on you, Stell, so don't let me down."

Folding the letter, she pushed it behind the milk jug. Where on earth did Adrian think she could so easily find two hundred pounds? She only had it at the moment because she hadn't spent a penny of her dress allowance, but even if the position between herself and Matthew had been normal, she would not have asked him to settle her brother's debts. How dare Adrian regard it so lightly; as if it were usual for a boy of nineteen to owe such a large amount of money.

At first she debated whether to ignore his plea for a few weeks, but afraid he would resort to further gambling, she sent him a cheque immediately, at the same time writing a firm and unsympathetic letter.

"If it weren't for worrying Mother, I'd refuse to help you. You're not a child any longer, and it's time you stood on your own feet. Matthew would be disgusted if he knew, so I'm sending the money out of my allowance. You'd better concentrate on your work while you're at the Academy. You may not always have someone behind you to help."

That was certainly true. Once she left Matthew she would not let Adrian accept any more help from him. If only she had never agreed to it in the first place!

Since their quarrel she and Matthew had never been alone together. At dinner he would talk politely to her and Jess, and as soon as the meal was over would retire to the study with his coffee-cup in his hand.

Jess tried to disguise her curiosity, and it was not until the day Adrian's letter arrived that she came into the open with her suspicions, eyeing Stella intently over the tea-trolley as they sat together in the drawing-room.

"You must have had a proper row with Matt to upset him so much. I've never known him to carry on like this."

"Like what?"

"Like pretending he has to work each evening. You've had more than a lover's tiff."

"I'd rather not discuss it. It's between Matthew and myself."

Jess sniffed. "He's not so careful about hiding it."

"What is that supposed to mean?"

"I could return the compliment and say I'd rather not discuss it! But I'm not such a lady as you. If I see Matt making a fool of himself I want to know why!"

"What are you getting at?" Stella set down her cup. "You're determined to tell me sooner or later, so why not now?"

"All right, I will." The large jaw jutted closer. "You've had a row and you're paying him back the way women usually do!"

"Really!"

"Don't really me. We're both married women so we know what's what. Trouble is, *you* don't know Matt. He's a hot-blooded man, and if you won't have him, he'll find someone who will!"

Stella's scalp prickled. This was plain speaking with a vengeance. "I'd rather not talk about it."

"Then you're a fool. If you let Belle get Matt . . ."

"You *know* her?" The question came of its own volition and Jess nodded, her eyes bright with malice.

"Matt was friendly with her years ago, and he's gone back to her now he's fed up with you."

"I wouldn't jump to conclusions so quickly," Stella retorted furiously. "The boot might be on the other foot."

Jess stared at her for a moment, then laughed. "You almost had me fooled! I suppose it hurts your pride

125

that you couldn't keep your husband more than three months! It must be hard to have him go to someone else so soon. Whatever was wrong with my Tom, you couldn't have said that about him."

"I wouldn't have even if I could!"

An ugly flush darkened Jess's face. "Thanks for the sermon, but I don't like seeing Matt act the fool."

Resolutely Stella maintained her silence, and after a glance in her direction, Jess went on talking.

"Belle's a good-looking girl, I'll say that for her. And not a money-grabber either."

"You seem to know her well." Anger prodded Stella's remark but the sarcasm went over Jess's head.

"Her older sister went to school with me. That's how Matt met her. She'd make some man a good wife, if she'd a mind to it. But she's never wanted to settle down. Always off with the old and on with the new! I often —"

The sound of a car brought her to a stop, and a moment later Matthew came into the room.

"Hullo, Stella." He turned to his sister. "Is the tea still hot?"

"No, I'll make another pot. You're early — anything wrong?"

"I just had a bellyful of work and decided to knock off."

Jess picked up the tray. "Close the door behind me. I won't be long."

Matthew did so, then crossed to the hearth and sat down opposite his wife. His wife! What a misnomer that was — what a mockery of all his hopes! At one time he would have said that no man in his right mind could go on desiring a woman who despised him, yet he wanted Stella as much now as he had ever done. She looked so pretty as she sat in front of the fire, the vivid green of her dress throwing her hair and face into relief. Damn it, why couldn't she understand him — why couldn't she see what had led him to go to Belle?

He took out his cigarette-case and offered her one. "No thanks. I've just put one out."

"It's never stopped you before." He flicked his lighter open. "That's a nice dress you've been wearing."

"You needn't be polite, Matthew — we've no audience."

He clenched his jaw. "I didn't say it for effect. It's smarter than the others you've been wearing."

"It's a similar style."

"But a different colour. I prefer you in bright ones."

"I'm not interested in your preferences."

"Whether you are or not, I like my wife to look smart!" His tone was sharp. "We've been invited to Milly and Ned's again — they're having some American cousins to dinner and I want you to buy yourself a new dress."

"I have my grey or black — I've hardly worn either of them."

"Get something gayer. You haven't spent a penny of the allowance I gave you last month."

"I don't consider it necessary to impress Milly and Ned."

He exhaled deliberately. "I want to feel proud of you in public."

"It's a good thing I don't want the same of you!"

"What does that mean?"

She shrugged. "I could hardly be proud of a husband who runs around with an old flame!"

He studied the tip of his shoe. "When you leave, I want my friends to think it was my fault. It won't matter if they feel sorry for *you*. A few months from now and you'll never see them again. But *I've* got to go on living here and I'd rather get no sympathy than too much. This way, they'll say I shouldn't have married you in the first place."

"I'm surprised you did. Belle would have made a

much better choice!"

He caught his breath, but when he spoke, his voice was calm. "I wanted to be the first man in my wife's life."

She shifted her gaze. "Perhaps you'll change your mind now."

"I might at that. She's warm and kind."

"So I understand."

"I wonder if you do." His eyes narrowed. "How did you know I'd been seeing her?"

"Jess made it her business to tell me."

A flicker of annoyance passed over his face, but further conversation was forestalled by Jess coming back with the tray.

"Sorry I've been such a time. Will you have another cup now I've made it, Stella?"

"No thanks. I'm going to have a rest before dinner."

The door closed behind her and Matthew watched his sister pour out the tea.

"Why did you tell Stella you saw me with Belle?" he asked abruptly.

"If I hadn't, someone else would. And if you're daft enough to take her to the biggest hotel in Leeds . . . No man in his senses would do that if he wanted to keep it quiet!"

"That's beside the point. It was spiteful of you to tell her."

"Why should you care? If you can pick up with Belle again you can't have much feeling for Stella. Not that I blame you. She's a —"

"When I want your opinion I'll ask for it!"

"You can have it without asking! What's wrong with you, Matt? I didn't think your marriage would last, but I never believed *you'd* be the one to break it up. Haven't you any shame? Don't you care what people will say?"

"At least they won't be sorry for me. When Stella goes, they'll say I deserved it."

Uncertainly, Jess regarded him. "I don't follow you."

"Stella would have left me, Belle or no Belle," he said heavily.

"I see. So it was like that." She stood up. "Poor Matt, you're no different from other men. Most of 'em would rather be thought immoral than rejected! When I think of that stuck-up little —"

"That's enough," he said wearily. "Go and see about dinner. I could do with something to eat."

CHAPTER TEN

STELLA racked her brains how to buy the new clothes Matthew wanted without having to ask him for the money. The two hundred pounds she had sent Adrian had swallowed her entire allowance and if she asked him for more she would have to tell him the reason. The only solution was to order the dresses on credit and settle the bills with her next quarter's allowance. Matthew wanted her to look smart and she would certainly not give him cause to complain of her appearance again! Brighter colours made her look more attractive, and inconsequentially she wondered what Belle was like, curious to see the woman to whom Matthew had gone. What would have happened if he had come home that night and accepted her offer to start again? Would they have been happy, or would their marriage — like so many others not founded on mutual love — have petered out into boredom? But it was useless to think about the might-have-been; what was done could not be undone.

For the next few days Matthew was more than usually morose, and Stella sensed he had quarrelled with his sister. One evening during dinner it struck her as incongruous that they should all sit in this over-furnished dining-room eating from the same table, yet having so little in common. What would her mother say if she knew she was living with a sister-in-law who ignored her and a husband who had turned to another woman?

She put down her fork and Matthew looked up.

"Haven't finished, have you?"

"I'm not hungry."

He resumed eating and she could not help thinking that a month ago he would have shown concern at her lack of appetite — would have made anxious suggestions that would have given her a feeling of being cared for; now he viewed the fact that she had scarcely eaten with calm unconcern. Disgruntled, she picked up her fork and began to peck at her food again.

There was a knock at the door and Elsie came in. "Someone to see you, Mr. Matthew. Says his name's Crowther and you're expecting him. I've put him in the study."

"That'll be the architect. Tell him I won't be long."

Jess looked enquiringly at her brother. "What do you want with an architect?"

"I'm building a new factory."

"Sudden, isn't it?"

"I've been thinking about it a long while. It'll be the most modern one in the country. Increase our production by two hundred per cent."

"Aren't you rich enough?" Stella asked.

"Once you're in my sort of position," Matthew said dryly, "you don't work for what you can earn. You work because it's a challenge, because you want to be better than anyone else, more efficient, show bigger profits. But there's no personal gain involved."

"You would still get richer though," she pointed out.

"The government would," he replied. "In *my* tax bracket I'm working for them!" He rose. "I'll not be seeing you again this evening, Stella. I'm going out when I've finished with Crowther."

The door closed behind him and Jess snorted. "How can you sit back and let him go to someone else night after night? Even if you don't love him, haven't you any pride?"

"I'd rather not discuss it."

"That's your favourite answer! But at least tell me one thing: did you like Matt at all when you married him or was it *only* because of his money?"

With something akin to despair Stella wondered

131

how much more cross-examination she would have to tolerate. "I'd every intention of making Matthew happy when I married him," she said quietly. "Unfortunately things went wrong from the start."

"Meaning no honeymoon and such like, I suppose?"

"That, and — and other things."

Jess sniffed. "I daresay it *would* affect someone like you. But the glamour would have worn off honeymoon or not, and then where would you have been? Right where you are now! I always suspected there was more to your marrying Matt than met the eye, though I must say you keep your reasons well hidden."

"What did you expect me to do — buy Harrods?"

Jess reddened. "You think you're very clever, don't you? But people here aren't as stupid as you make out. Do you think they don't know why you never bother getting dressed up when you go out? Not because you don't want to show off, but because you *are* showing off! Because you think you're so much better than everyone else that being smart isn't necessary!"

"Of all the ridiculous . . ." Words failed her, and Stella longed to wipe the smug smile off the ugly face so close to her own. But she was determined not to enter into a slanging match, knowing that a reasoned reply would arouse more fury than a show of anger. "I'm sorry if my trousseau hasn't met with your approval. Obviously we don't have the same taste."

"You've none at all. Half the time you look as if you're going to a funeral! The only time you got dressed up was when your fancy friend came to dinner. Nothing was too much trouble for him! You filled the house with flowers and expensive food and spent money like water. But anything's good enough for Matt!"

"You're in charge of the housekeeping," Stella

said icily. "You've made that abundantly clear."

The sharpness of the retort was blunted by Jess' thick skin. "That still shouldn't stop you from being a loving wife. I've never even seen you kiss him!"

"I wouldn't in front of you!"

"Hoity-toity!"

Clenching her hands, Stella held back the urge to smack the smug red face. "I'm going to bed," she said tightly.

"When are you going properly? To London, I mean. Matt said you'd be leaving soon."

"Then ask *him* for the date," she said and slammed the door behind her.

Towards the end of the week Stella went to Leeds and spent the day shopping. Matthew wanted her to be well dressed, so she would comply with his order. At least she would have a chance to see if Jess enjoyed watching someone else spend her brother's money!

At the big stores the assistants were eager to serve her, taking it for granted as soon as she mentioned her name that the goods were to be charged to Matthew's account, and although she had only intended buying a couple of dresses she returned home laden with parcels.

Jess was in the hall as she came in. "Well, well, you've done yourself proud! Wouldn't be wanting any help to get that lot upstairs, would you?" she enquired sarcastically.

"Thanks." Stella's tone was laconic. "You can bring up the three boxes in the porch, if you like."

With a muttered exclamation Jess disappeared into the kitchen and Stella went upstairs smiling.

Milly's dinner-party was the first occasion she would be seen in public with Matthew since his name had been linked with Belle's, and though she had professed disinterest in what his friends thought, she dreaded having to face them. Once they had envied

133

her for having married him; now they would pity her for the same reason.

She dressed for the event as carefully as for the evening with Charles, and when she went downstairs was conscious of looking her best. Her hair had been set into a high coronet on top of her head and her make-up was more accentuated than usual, eyelashes and eyelids darkened, lips softly pink to match the lacquer on her nails. In deference to Matthew's liking for vivid colours she wore a dress of peacock blue with a tightly swathed bodice and full skirt. As she and Matthew were the same height she rarely put on high heels, but now she did, and her silver sandals together with her upswept hair made her appear even taller than she was. He had once called her his star, the woman he set on a pedestal; if the idol had proved to have feet of clay, at least he should still look up to her!

Coming into the drawing-room a few minutes later, Matthew stared at her in surprise, but the coldness of her eyes belied the provocation of her loveliness.

"You're punctual, Matthew."

"Not more than you."

He walked across and stood in front of the fire, the grey hair at his temples catching the light. In a dinner jacket he looked commanding and impressive, and it was hard to believe he had ever held her in his arms and been so humbled by his love.

Quickly she reached out for her coat but he took it from her and silently held it out. For a moment his hands lingered on the fur and she trembled at their pressure and drew quickly away, relieved to hear Jess's step across the hall.

Entering Milly's living room some half hour later, Stella was acutely conscious of the hush that greeted them, and she clung tightly to her hostess' hand.

"I'm so pleased you came early," the woman smiled and led her over to the bar.

Stella was reminded of her first visit here. Then she had been toasted as a bride: now it was only a matter of weeks before she would become a runaway wife.

Aware of Ned's speculative gaze she forced herself to an unusual gaiety and deliberately stayed close to Matthew, joining in the conversation whenever she could.

"How's the new factory going?" Ned asked him suddenly.

"I approved the plans last week. It's going to be the best —"

"Factory in Yorkshire," Stella interrupted. "But you promised you wouldn't talk business tonight and I'm going to keep you to your word." She gave Ned a melting glance. "Matthew works so hard during the day that I insist he relaxes at night."

Ned beamed. "My wife's been trying to make me do that for years."

"Trying what?" Milly asked vaguely.

"To make me stop talking shop when I'm home. Stella's trying to do it with Matt."

Milly smiled. "Any luck?"

"Not much. I don't see enough of him for it to take effect." Stella slipped her arm through Matthew's and felt him stiffen at her touch. "I'm on my own so much in the evenings that I told him I'd complain to his friends — perhaps you'll have more influence on him than I have!"

Milly laughed. "Husbands take a long time to train, my dear, but it's worth persevering. Now let's go in to dinner, shall we?"

On their way across the hall Matthew drew her aside. "What are you trying to do?" he whispered furiously. "All this talk about being alone at night — what d'you want people to think?"

"Only what *you* want them to," she said innocently.

"I thought you'd like me to give the impression that I minded being on my own."

"You needn't overdo the act," he growled.

"But it's for your sake. You want your friends to believe I love you, and after tonight I'm sure they will!"

Driving home several hours later Stella knew she had created the impression she had wanted. After tonight no one would be able to say she was an unloving wife: her openly adoring looks at Matthew had seen to that. With wry amusement she wondered how Jess had viewed her behaviour, and as soon as they entered the house her sister-in-law gave vent to her opinion.

"I don't know what your game was, but you played it perfectly!"

"Thank you, Jess, a word of praise from you is rare indeed."

"I didn't intend it as praise," the woman snorted, and stumped upstairs as her brother came in and closed the door.

In the dim light of the hall Stella was aware of the powerful width of his shoulders, and as he moved towards her she felt a tremor of fear.

"Not only did you look the part of the adoring wife," he said heavily, "but you acted it well too!"

"The Armstrong family are in a very complimentary mood tonight — your sister's just said the same thing."

"But Jess couldn't appreciate it like me! It was interesting to see how you could have been if you'd had a mind. Let's see what you're like without an audience."

Before she realized his intention his arms closed around her and his mouth came down on hers. Matthew had kissed her before with passion, with tenderness, with force, but never so completely the master of his own emotions or so regardless of hers, and she swayed against him, her lips responding of their own volition until the kiss had spent itself.

He let her go and she stared at him dumbly. Until now he had always been the one who was uncertain: this time it was she who could find nothing to say.

"You'd better go to bed," he said quietly. "The curtain's down."

Still without speaking she went up the stairs, but though her head was high her lips were trembling.

As soon as she awoke the following morning Stella's thoughts flew to Matthew. His kiss had shown her, as nothing else could, that he was not the same man she had known in London. It had been a selfish kiss with a strange quality of detachment, and where a few months ago she would have ridiculed the idea of his caring for anyone else, now she was not so sure. Matthew had been the one person on whom she had thought she could depend and with feminine perversity she felt cheated that she could no longer take his devotion for granted.

Irritably she sat up in bed, forcing herself to smile as Elsie came in with her tray. On it was a letter from Adrian, and the smile left her face as she read its contents. It was almost identical to his last one, though this time he made no excuse for wanting more money, merely saying he was in debt again and needed help.

Shaking with nerves, she pushed aside her tray. She had intended using her next allowance to pay the bills she had incurred, but if she sent Adrian the money, the unpaid accounts would go to Matthew. And she couldn't let that happen! If it did, he would want to know what she had done with her allowance, and to lie to him would be impossible. One look at her face and he would know she was hiding something. No, her only hope of covering up for her brother was to raise the money he needed by selling something. But what? Apart from her engagement

137

ring — which she daren't sell — her only possession of value was the diamond watch Matthew had given her on their wedding day, and loath though she was to part with it, she had no choice.

Anger against Adrian mounted. How dare he write and demand money again? Didn't he have any sense of gratitude to Matthew — even to herself — for giving him a chance to follow the career he had set his heart on? This was the last time she would help him. From now on he must stand or fall by his own efforts.

Later that day she took a bus into Leeds, wearing the most inconspicuous clothes in her wardrobe. Avoiding the large jewellers she walked the length of Brig-gate before finding a discreet but well-established firm of family silversmiths.

The man behind the counter appraised the watch and made no comment on her story that it had been left to her in an aunt's will. He excused himself and disappeared into an inner room, and for a moment Stella panicked at the idea that he might think she had stolen it. However he returned and put the watch down on the counter.

"The best offer we can make is ninety pounds."

"It's worth far more than that!"

"Possibly, but we've a very small sale for this sort of thing. It would have to be cleaned — and —"

"But it's practically new! I — I mean, my aunt bought it just before she died."

He looked at her curiously but said nothing, and a few minutes later Stella left the shop with the money in her handbag. Going straight to the post office, she bought a money order for the entire amount, and, standing in a little booth, penned a letter to Adrian.

"I had to sell my diamond watch to get you this, and it's the last time I intend helping you. If you get in debt again, don't bother coming to me."

She tapped the pen against her cheek, debating whether to tell him she was leaving Matthew, then decided to give him a hint.

"Make the most of your time at the Academy, for Matthew may not be behind you much longer. He's generous at the moment, but don't bank on it lasting."

With the money despatched, she put her brother from her mind, but it was not as easy to forget how she had obtained it. Memory of Matthew's pleasure when he had given her the watch kept haunting her, increasing the guilt she had felt at having to part with it. It seemed wrong for Adrian to benefit from it, and when the only acknowledgement of her letter was a curt note of thanks, she was dismally aware that as a brother he fell lamentably short of her expectations.

If Stella had not been preoccupied with Adrian her days would have been unbearably empty. Jess became increasingly taciturn and Matthew was out all day and most evenings. Pride forbade her asking him about the new factory, and the first news she had of its progress was when he told her he wanted her to lay the foundation stone.

"The men will expect it, so we may as well make it an occasion. It'll be the last one we'll be able to give them before you go."

"Will I have to make a speech?"

"Just a few words — I'll write it for you. The main thing is to be smart and pretty and look as if you cared."

She flushed at his tone. "Must you be so rude? Anyone would think *I* had broken our marriage!"

"It was finished before I went to Belle, if that's what you mean. You showed your opinion of me quite plainly when Charles came to dinner." His face was expressionless, but there was more emotion in his voice than she had heard for a long time. "I'll

139

never forget how you behaved when I asked you to play for me."

"I apologized for that," she said awkwardly. "Can't you forget it?"

"Can you forget Belle?"

"That's different."

"Is it? One hurt my pride as much as the other hurt yours."

"You flatter yourself," she retorted. "Nothing you could do would hurt me."

He rubbed the side of his face wearily. "I suppose not, but I hope for your sake you'll find a man who *will* be able to hurt you. Otherwise you'll go through life without any love at all. Now let's drop the subject. I'll go and write your speech."

It was after dinner one evening towards the end of the week that Matthew asked to speak to her privately, and preceding him into the study she thought how well the room suited him, with its cheerful modern atmosphere and rich smell of leather. In his own background he looked masterful and commanding, and she could understand the respect with which he was regarded by everyone who worked for him. Seeing him like this it was easy to appreciate his attraction, to be swayed by the virile magnetism that emanated from his every gesture.

Eyes fixed on him, she leaned against the side of an armchair. "What do you want to talk to me about?"

"Don't you know? Or do you intend to brazen it out? I wouldn't try, if I were you."

His menacing tone took her by surprise. "I don't know what you mean."

"Don't put on an act with me!"

"I'm not. What are you talking about?"

"The watch!" he shouted. "That's what I'm talking about!" He banged his hand on the desk. "If you needed more money for clothes why didn't you ask me for it? Or did you want to humiliate me by selling the present I gave you?"

He flung the diamond watch on to the blotter, and seeing it, her face flamed. "I didn't . . . I didn't think you would find out. I'm sorry."

"I bet you are!"

"How did you get it? I never gave the jeweller my real name."

"I went there to buy a present for Belle," he said bluntly, "and they offered me this. It was lucky I hadn't bought it there in the first place — that would have made me look a real fool!" He came round the side of his desk. "You couldn't have spent your whole allowance on the clothes you bought. Why did you need more?"

She avoided his eyes. "I had a reason . . . it's private."

"Selling my present was very public though, so I'd like an answer."

"Can't you forget it?"

"No."

"It's none of your business," she said desperately.

"Everything you do is my business," he retorted, his anger rising visibly. "What are you hiding? What are you frightened to tell me?"

Her longing to blurt out the truth died in the face of his fury. In his present mood he might easily stop Adrian's allowance entirely. And she couldn't let that happen. At least not until she had spoken to Adrian herself and made arrangements — though heaven alone knew how she would do it — to pay his fees herself.

"Well," Matthew said violently. "I'm waiting for an answer and I won't let you go until I get one."

"Then you'll have to keep me a prisoner here! I've no intention of telling you and shouting won't make me. The watch was mine and I had a right to sell it if I wanted to."

"You wanted the money for someone else," he grated. "You didn't spend it on yourself. I'm not fool enough to believe that."

"I don't care what you believe! You've no right to shout at me like this. I'm not your slave."

"You're not my anything — except a disloyal, deceitful woman!"

He slumped down in a chair, his anger replaced by a weariness that left him looking more dejected than she had ever seen him before.

Watching him, Stella's own anger disappeared and she was overcome by remorse. Poor Matthew. She had robbed him of every illusion he had cherished about her, and had left him nothing but regret and bitterness.

"Matthew," she whispered, "I want to —"

"Get out," he said softly. "Get out of my sight."

It was not until much later that evening that Stella's remorse ebbed sufficiently for her to remember exactly how Matthew had discovered she had sold the watch, and with the knowledge her remorse vanished. So he had gone to buy a present for another woman. It served him right to get a shock! Pity she couldn't give him a few more. What right did he have to complain she was making a fool of him when he was doing exactly the same to her?

Angrily she tried to get to sleep, but memory of the bitter scene kept her nerves at fever pitch. What sort of girl was Belle to be able to hold his interest for so long? To make him return to her for sympathy and love? Love. Stella trembled at the mention of the word, her imagination giving it reality, so that her mind's eye could visualize him kissing willing lips, touching an eager body.

"I must be mad!" Spoken aloud, the words restored her to some semblance of calm, but sleep still would not come and she sat up in bed and turned on the light. She did not know if Matthew was home.

In the past few weeks, since Jess had learned the truth about them, he no longer occupied the dressing room, sleeping instead in a corner bedroom on the other side of the hall. Was he also regretting their quarrel she wondered, or was he still too angry to realise she might have a perfectly good reason for not telling him what he wanted to know?

Perhaps in the morning she would tell him the whole story, tell him too that she had warned Adrian she would not help him any more. At least it would show Matthew she did not condone her brother's behaviour, nor expect the boy to go on being helped if he did not have the sense to help himself.

Not falling asleep till dawn, it was midday when she awoke, and only then because Elsie came in with a telegram. It was from Charles. He was on his way north and would be calling to see her that evening.

"Not bad news, ma'am?" Elsie asked anxiously.

"I don't think so. Mr. Hayward's coming this evening. I'm sure if there was anything wrong he would have telephoned."

"What would you like for dinner? Miss Jess has gone to Cleethorpes for a few days."

Stella bit her lip. How like her sister-in-law to go away without even the courtesy of telling her.

"She left cold mutton and pork," Elsie went on, "but if you'd like to leave it to me . . ."

Stella grinned. "I'd be delighted!"

"Then we'll have fresh salmon. I'll leave everything ready in the dining-room and cover it with a cloth. Then you can help yourself. There'll only be the two of you. Mr. Matthew isn't in to dinner."

Some of Stella's good humour evaporated. It was ironical that she knew less about her husband's movements than Elsie.

"He's having a snack with the architect," the girl continued. "I heard him tell Miss Jess. Then he's going to the site."

Her pleasure in knowing Matthew would not be with Belle filled Stella with such happiness that she was afraid. Why should she care *what* he did so long as he did not bother her?

"Perhaps we can leave him some hot soup in a flask?" she was surprised to hear herself say. "He'll need warming up when he comes in."

"Barley soup," Elsie said. "Mr. Matthew loves that. It's nice to be on our own, isn't it?"

"Yes," Stella smiled, and pondered on the remark long after the girl had left the room. If she and Matthew could have started their marriage the way they had planned, instead of having to begin it under Jess's disapproving eye, so many things might have been different. No lonely hours waiting for him to come home that first night; no business problems to turn him into a stranger; no Belle . . .

Belle. The thought of this unknown yet pervasive woman abruptly brought Stella back to the present. It was pointless to go on with these thoughts. The past could not be altered and, because of it, nor could the future.

With Jess out of the house Grey Walls seemed less oppressive, and Stella enjoyed wandering through the rooms and moving the furniture into different positions. The ugly Knowle suite looked less stiff when pulled away from the walls and set informally in front of the hearth, and the dining table, opened to it's full length, became long and graceful instead of squat and truncated.

It was nine o'clock before Charles arrived, apologizing profusely for being late and blaming it on heavy traffic along the motorway.

"I had to come by car," he explained. "There were so many things to do before I left that I couldn't rely on catching a train."

"Is anything wrong?" she questioned. "You look awfully pale."

"Haven't you seen the papers?"

"Not for a couple of days. Why?"

"Uncle Henry and Alan were drowned during the weekend. Their boat capsised off the coast."

Stella sat down. "How ghastly."

"Yes," he said jerkily. "It was a terrible shock. I can't believe it even now." He rubbed a hand over his forehead. "I'm on my way north for the funeral, but I — I wanted to see you first."

She stood up quickly. "Let's eat something. You look as if you can do with it."

"I could do with a drink."

"Of course, how stupid of me."

Chattering the whole time she poured him a whisky, keeping up the conversation as they went into the dining room. But with the meal finished, and sitting opposite him in the drawing-room again, she knew she could no longer stave off what he had come here to say.

"Even you can't talk forever," he said dryly. "Though you made a very good try." He clasped his hands together, calm and judicial, only the tenseness around his eyes giving him away. "Since I saw you last I haven't been able to get you out of my mind. You were so on edge — so unhappy."

"I'd quarrelled with Matthew over his sister," she said hastily. "That was why."

"It went deeper than that. I'm not blind, Stella. At one time I thought you liked Armstrong more than you would admit, but after seeing the two of you that night . . ." He leaned forward. "Don't pretend with me anymore. After all these years you at least owe me honesty."

She stared at the carpet, wondering at her own indecision and the welter of conflicting emotions that had taken possession of her. "I don't know what to say," she whispered. "And that's being as honest as I can! Things aren't working out between Matthew

145

and me, but that doesn't mean . . . I'm still married to him, Charles. I'm still his wife."

"But you don't love him! You've nothing in common and you should never have married him in the first place! Not that I blame you entirely. I was just as much at fault for not stopping you."

"You tried," she reminded him.

"Not strongly enough. It wasn't because I didn't love you — you know that — but because I couldn't give you what you wanted." He jumped up and came over to her. "But now I can! I can help Adrian and your mother and do everything Armstrong's doing! Don't turn me down. You love me, Stella. We're the same kind of people and we should have married years ago."

"But we didn't. Talking like this won't turn back the clock."

"Then push the hands forward! Think of the future — our future. We'll be so happy, Stella! We'll be able to do everything we've ever wanted. No more slogging in an office for me and you won't need to bury yourself miles from everyone who cares for you! Leave Armstrong. Leave him and come to me."

"How can you talk like this? He's my husband! What's got into you, Charles? Haven't you any sense of decency!"

There was a short, ugly silence, and Stella wished she could retract the words. "I'm sorry. I shouldn't have said that. But you took me by surprise."

"I always seem to surprise you," he said bleakly. "Either I'm too reserved for you or I'm too emotional." He paused, then said: "When I heard about my uncle and cousin I didn't know where I was. I couldn't take it all in. Then I realised what it meant to us . . . that we could be together . . . so I had to come and see you."

Sadly she looked at him, knowing she could not give him the answer he wanted. "It's no good,

Charles. I can't marry you. I couldn't, even if I were free."

"I've given you a shock." He spoke as if he had not heard her. "You can't take it in either."

"That's not true. Please don't fool yourself, it won't do any good. I *can't* marry you."

"Of course you can! If all this had happened earlier, you wouldn't have hesitated. You're being unnecessarily loyal. Armstrong married you knowing you didn't love him and —"

"That doesn't mean I can cheat him twice!"

"You're cheating him by staying with him! He's no fool. He knows what you think of him."

"How can he know when I don't know myself!"

"Stella!" Shocked, Charles stared at her. "You feel sorry for Armstrong. Nothing more than that. And even your sympathy's wasted! He knew you married him to help your family and he accepted you on those terms."

"And now I don't need him — now *you* can take up where he leaves off — you suggest I leave him?"

"Certainly. It's the logical thing to do."

Her laugh was harsh. "You're as selfish and unloving as I am!"

"If that's meant to be funny . . ."

"It's not funny at all. It's tragic."

"I never expected you to act like this," Charles burst out. "I don't know what's got into you."

"I don't know either." Wearily she rested her head in her hands. "Do you mind if we don't talk about it anymore. I *will* be leaving Matthew but I don't know what I'll do afterwards. I don't even want to think beyond the next few months."

"Very well." As though satisfied that he had won his point, Charles was his old, gentle self. "I don't care how long I have to wait for you. Just remember I'll always be there."

His words reminded her that Matthew had once

said the same. Yet how quickly he had forgotten, turning to someone else the first time they had quarrelled. Her eyes strayed to the piano, and remembering the last time she had played for him, she could not find it in her heart to blame him. Like a wounded animal he had turned for comfort to the one person who could give it to him.

Sympathy for Matthew overflowed towards Charles, making her hold out her hands to him. "Dear Charles, I'm not worth your loving."

"I'm the best judge of that."

Unexpectedly he pulled her to her feet and kissed her. Passively she surrendered to the gentle pressure of his lips, not wanting to hurt him by showing the distaste — almost revulsion — she felt at having his arms around her.

"Stella," he muttered, "I love you. Come away with me."

"Not till *I've* finished with her!"

With an exclamation Charles drew back, horrified to see Matthew in the doorway, his face twisted with fury.

"Get out of my house!" Matthew ordered. "Get out before I kill you!"

Throwing Stella an anxious look Charles moved close to her again, but she shook her head at him, her eyes pleading.

"You'd better go, Charles. Quickly."

Silently he obeyed her. The front door slammed, his car engine reved and then faded into the distance. Only then did she glance at Matthew, frightened by his flushed face and red rimmed eyes.

"There's no need to look so angry," she said as coolly as she could. "He was only — only kissing me goodbye."

"And asking you to go with him at the same time! Don't bother pretending with me. I know what game you're playing at."

He lurched towards her and she stepped behind the settee, her heart pounding. "You're drunk!"

"Not so drunk that I don't know when I'm being made a fool of! Letting your fancy friend make love to you when my back's turned! You weren't so cold when he held you in his arms, were you — or aren't you as particular as you used to be?" He reached out and pulled her towards him. "He was the one you wanted the money for, wasn't it? Your friend Charles didn't have enough money to marry you, so you married a fool who could help him instead? I've been looking after your brother and you've been looking after your boy friend!"

"That's not true! I've never given him money and you know it!"

"Do I?" he sneered. "Well, I don't know it any longer! If you can kiss him like that you can kiss me — and more! I've a greater right than anyone else — I'm your husband, or have you forgotten it?" She tried to push past him but he barred her way. "No, you don't. You're not getting away from me this time, my lovely Stella! Let's see how lovely you can be to the poor fool who married you!"

He caught her close, forcing her head back as she struggled in his grasp. "No Matthew, no! You don't know what you're doing!"

"It's the first time I do!" he said harshly. "I should have done this a long time ago. If I had, you'd be different to what you are now — cold, heartless, dishonest, unwomanly! The only thing you've never been is a wife!"

Her protests were stifled as his lips crushed down on hers, and her limbs weakened against the hard pressure of his body. She pressed her hands against his chest but her strength was puny against his, and, though she tried to turn her head away, his would not leave hers. Never had any man assaulted her senses like this, never had she been kissed with such naked passion. She reeled against him, half fainting as he picked her up in his arms, kicked open the door and climbed the stairs.

naked passion. She reeled against him, half fainting
as he picked her up. His arms kicked open the

CHAPTER ELEVEN

SENSING that someone was watching her, Stella
stirred and opened her eyes, colour flooding her face
as she saw Matthew standing at the foot of the bed.
They looked at one another in silence, then with a
groan he sat down and buried his head in his hands.

"What have you done to me? What kind of man
have you made me?" Still she said nothing, and he
raised his head. "Until last night I had my self-respect.
Now I haven't even got that."

"I didn't rob you of it," she said quietly.

His hands lifted in a hopeless gesture. "I've no
excuse to offer, except that when I saw you with
Charles I went mad."

"Charles was kissing me against my will — there
was nothing between us and there never has been.
As for my giving him money, the question never
arose because he never needed it."

"You don't owe me any explanations," he said
gruffly.

"But I *want* you to know! Charles wasn't in your
sort of position, but he wasn't on the bread line
either! And he certainly isn't now! His uncle and
cousin died a few days ago and he's the sole heir.
If you had let me explain . . ."

"I was crazy with temper," Matthew muttered.
"When I saw him holding you I couldn't think
straight."

"I suppose you think I sold my watch for Charles
too? Well I didn't. It was for Adrian. He'd been
gambling and he needed the money."

"I should have guessed." With a groan Matthew
got to his feet. "Why didn't you come to me?"

"And ask you for *more* money? I owed you too
much already."

"After last night, you owe me nothing. I'm the one who owes *you*. I did something I'll regret for the rest of my life — something I can never put right." His voice was anguished. "It would be better for both of us if you left. You won't be able to look at me without remembering and I'll never be able to look at you and forget."

"Very well."

"Is that all you can say?"

"What else is there?"

She closed her eyes, and when she opened them again he had gone. Miserably she got out of bed and began to dress. Matthew had done her the greatest wrong a man could do to a woman, but she was unable to hate him, unable to forget that, as he had overcome her defences, so he had overcome her fear of him until, forgetting all else, she had clung to him with abandon, no longer forcing him to conquer but willingly giving him what he desired.

Yet he did not seem to realise it! Battered by self-hatred he only remembered her first cries of anguish; he had forgotten her last cries of surrender. And because of this he had asked her to go.

Last night she had wept with shame, but the emotion she felt now was totally different, defying analysis and leaving her bewildered and frightened. She stared at herself in the full length mirror, marvelling that there was no difference to be seen in her tall, slender figure; nothing to indicate the frenzy it had aroused in Matthew. Hastily she averted her gaze, forcing her mind back to the present and, inevitably, towards the future.

Coming out of the bathroom she found Elsie waiting with her breakfast tray.

"You shouldn't have bothered to bring it up," she protested. "You have quite enough to do."

"I like looking after you," the girl said, blushing.

152

"You're always so polite and — and friendly. Not a bit stuck up!"

Knowing she was hearing Jess's opinion of herself Stella could not help a wry smile.

"Will you be leaving the supper to me?" Elsie went on. "I thought I'd make a cheese souffle to begin with."

"That sounds fine," Stella spoke automatically, wondering whether or not to tell Elsie she would not be here. Yet something prevented her from doing so, and sipping her coffee she was overcome by such a sense of commitment, that she knew she could not leave today. She had promised Matthew she would lay the foundation stone of his new factory and she intended to keep her word.

For the rest of the day she forced herself to find things to do. As always when Jess was out of the house the atmosphere lightened, and without a sense of interfering — which she usually felt when her sister-in-law was around — she helped Elsie with the dusting, filled the house with blossom laden branches and laid the table for dinner in the dining-room.

"If you could ring up and find out what time Mr. Matthew will be home," Elsie said, "I'd know when to put the souffle in the oven."

Reluctant to make the call Stella hedged. She had never rung Matthew at his office, and it would be embarrassing to do so now, when he expected her to be halfway to London. But at six o'clock she telephoned the factory gates, and learned that Matthew's car had just left.

"Then we can have dinner at seven," Elsie said happily. "Is that all right with you?"

Stella nodded and hurried to her room to change, wondering why she should be so nervous at seeing Matthew. The intimacy of last night had been so fleeting that it was almost as if it had never happened.

Yet it had. And because of it she would never be the same. She had once read that a woman always remembered the first man who had possessed her. If this were true then the memory of Matthew would stay with her for ever.

Forcing herself not to think of this she ran downstairs, and was crossing the hall when he came through the front door. He stared in surprise as he saw her. For a long moment they stared at one another. His face was so colourless that the stubble on his cheeks seemed darker, making him look unexpectedly older and tired. His heavy overcoat appeared to weigh him down, for his broad shoulders sagged and his hands hung limply at his sides, but as she watched him his shoulders straightened and his fists clenched, making him look more like his pugnacious self.

"I thought you would be in London by now."

"I agreed to lay the foundation-stone for you, and I'll keep my word."

"There was no need. I didn't expect you to. As I said this morning, after what — after last night you owe me nothing."

She shrugged. "I promised. Anyway, a few days either way won't make any difference."

He looked about to reply but changed his mind. "I'll go out for dinner then."

"There's no need. We're surely adult enough to be able to dine together."

"I didn't think you . . . Seeing me must —"

"Please," she interrupted, "let's not talk about it. Dinner's at seven."

"I'll be ready."

Sitting opposite him in the dining-room Stella made an effort to keep up a conversation but Matthew answered monosyllabically, avoiding her eyes and generally looking so uncomfortable that she was finally reduced to silence. Whom did he hate most, she wondered, her or himself? As though aware of what was

154

going through her mind he pushed aside his plate and abruptly got to his feet.

"Seems I'm not as sophisticated as you," he said jerkily. "In your position I wouldn't be talking to me at all!"

Slowly she set her fork on her plate, giving herself time to consider her answer. "Aren't you being old-fashioned about it? We *are* married, you know, and in the normal course of events . . ."

"Nothing's been normal with us! And you can't pretend last night was, either!"

She looked away, choosing her words with even more care. "I didn't fight you the whole time."

"I'm aware of that," he said heavily. "And it makes it worse. I've been thinking of nothing else all day. The way you suddenly gave in . . . the way you . . . But it makes me hate myself all the more!" He raised his hands and looked at them with loathing. "I forced you . . . you *had* to give in."

"I — I —" Half-formed sentences, like her half-formed thoughts, died in her throat, and she watched wordlessly as he strode to the door.

"I'm going out. I don't want anymore to eat."

Staring at the ruins of the meal, Stella decided it would have been better if she had returned to London that day. All she had accomplished by staying here was to make Matthew feel even more guilty towards her than he already did. Angrily she stacked the dishes and took them into the kitchen, forestalling Elsie.

"Don't bother serving the sweet," she said. "Mr. Matthew had to go out again."

"Won't you have some?"

Stella fought against her depression. "Yes, of course. A big helping, Elsie. I'm hungry."

Jess came back from Cleethorpes the following day. The change seemed to have done her good and she was more amiable than usual.

"I've got my outfit for the ceremony tomorrow," she confided over tea. "What are you wearing?"

"Either a suit or dress and coat — it depends on the weather."

"I hope it's fine, then. You look well in a suit; you've got the figure for it." Jess poured herself a second cup of tea. "Elsie said your friend was up again. He must like Leeds."

"He was going north to his uncle's funeral."

"Oh. Any money left him?"

The woman's bluntness demanded a blunt reply. "As a matter of fact, he's come into a fortune."

"Has he indeed! Pity it didn't happen before. He might have stood a better chance with you."

"For heaven's sake, don't pick a quarrel! At least let's be civil to each other till I go."

"You're quick to take offence! I didn't mean to rile you!"

"Then it's the first time you've done it unintentionally."

Jess bridled. "Your tongue's been sharpened while I've been away. May I ask *when* you're going?"

"The day after tomorrow."

"In that case we won't have to be civil for long."

Jess walked out and Stella went over to the piano. But after a few minutes she closed the lid and dropped her hands in her lap. What would happen at Grey Walls when she left? It hurt to know that after her departure everything would go on as if her marriage had never taken place. Matthew would forget her more quickly than she would forget him — for he would not *want* to remember her. But brooding would not change things, and with a sigh she wandered out to the garden to try and find something to do.

The following day was typical late spring, with a pale sun shining brightly over the garden. Matthew came home for an early lunch and at two o'clock they set out for the factory site. He drove the car himself, the speedometer creeping higher and higher until Jess remarked dourly that if he wanted to be summoned he was going the right way about it.

Stella was aware of his tension and longed for the ceremony to be over. "Are the men pleased you're building another factory?" she asked.

"Most of them. One or two aren't."

"Do you think they'll make trouble?"

"I'm not worried."

They drove through the southern outskirts of Leeds, passing the inevitable terraces of brick houses, goods yards and dingy pubs before coming out beyond the steel works and foundries to the wide stretch of road beyond.

Matthew waved a laconic hand. "That's my present factory. The new one's a couple of miles down the road."

She looked at the concrete buildings sprawling for hundreds of yards and felt a thrill of pride that this man should have achieved so much. "It's bigger than I thought. You must be proud of it."

"What's built can just as easily be destroyed," he said morosely.

Before she could think of a reply they approached the levelled site of the new factory and crowds of work people made a path for them. A platform had been erected to one side and several bulldozers, idle and muddy, stood in a phalanx at the far end. The workmen cheered and clapped as Matthew mounted the wooden steps with Stella at his side, and he stepped forward and acknowledged the applause with a wave of his hand.

She remembered little of the ceremony that followed, only aware of hundreds of pairs of eyes staring at her as the stone was swung into position and she tapped it with a small hammer. Reading the speech Matthew had written she was acutely conscious of the irony of the words he had given her to say, surprised at her own emotion as she spoke them.

"It has always been my husband's wish to build the most modern factory in the West Riding, for he believes that the prosperity of the country as a whole depends on the proper development of its industrial areas. For this reason he has planned this extension of his plant, and I am delighted to lay the foundation-stone and wish everyone who works here the best of luck and success."

Then it was over, and they made their way back to the car amid cheers and handshakes. Matthew stopped to speak to groups of men who stood along the path and had a special smile for a brigade of little boys lustily singing 'For He's a Jolly Good Fellow' with the tuneless bravado of the very young.

At last they reached the car, and as Matthew got into the driving-seat Ted put his head in at the window. "Glad everything went off so quietly, Matt. I heard this morning that a few of the gang were on the war-path." He turned to Jess. "How about coming home to tea with me? The wife asked me to bring you back."

"Thanks Ted, but I don't —"

"Come on, Jess!" He winked at Stella. "It's quite an occasion for Matt — leave him alone with his wife."

Jess reddened. "All right. But I can't stay long."

With a cheery wave Ted propelled her to his own car, and Matthew switched on the ignition and steered slowly over the rough path to the road.

Stella leaned back with a sigh of relief. "I'm glad that's over. I was nervous."

"You did very well. Thanks for staying to see it through."

"What did Ted mean about the gang being on the war-path?"

"Some of the men aren't pleased about the new

factory. There are always a few who have different ideas from the rest. He was afraid they'd start trouble."

"Thank heaven they didn't."

He shrugged. "I don't mind a fair fight. It's when people hit below the belt that I object."

Once again she felt the sting of his bitterness. "Even so, you're a born fighter. You'd never give in."

"Not if it was worth fighting for. Some things aren't."

They were nearing the old factory and she laid a hand on his arm. "Slow down a bit. I'd like to have a look at it."

He glanced at her in surprise but took his foot off the accelerator. She gazed curiously at the gaunt structures with their countless windows staring back at her like blind eyes. It was here that Matthew spent so much of his life, here that he had power and responsibilities, and once again she felt how much there was about him that she had failed to understand.

They passed the last building and he gathered speed. "Well, does it look as imposing at second sight?"

"Even more so. It's like a kingdom on its own."

"And I'm the dictator, I suppose?"

"I didn't mean that. I only meant that there's so much about you I hadn't realized before."

"Rather sudden, isn't it? I imagined —"

There was a sudden crash and a splintering of glass. "Matthew!" she screamed. "They're throwing bricks!"

But it was too late. A large missile came through the driving-window and with a groan Matthew slumped over the wheel.

Desperately she tried to push him off the steering column but he was too heavy to move and the car lurched drunkenly off the road, careened headlong up an incline and came to a shuddering halt with its nose buried in the bank. All the breath was knocked out of her body and she lay stunned, half off, half on the seat.

She was roused to conscious thought by an ominous crackling, and a spasm of terror gripped her as she saw tongues of flame licking the bonnet. Frantically she pulled at Matthew's arm, shouting his name, but he remained inert, and she raised his head from the wheel to see that his face was ashen except for a trickle of blood that ran across his forehead and down one cheek.

Wildly she pushed at the front doors, but they were both jammed and she clambered over the seat to try the rear ones. To her relief one of them gave way and she fell out on to the grass verge, the car lurching violently as her weight left it. Flames were already scorching the coach-work as she tugged at Matthew's door from the outside. Still the handle would not yield and she climbed back again and tried to pull him over the seat. Her muscles strained in their sockets but her strength was not equal to his weight, and feverishly she jumped down and ran to the far side to tug at the other door, sobbing with relief when it flew open.

It was even more difficult to pull Matthew out from this angle, and she had to drag him inch by inch across the seat. With his body half resting on the wheel he was heavy enough, but as she pulled him clear his full weight sagged against her and she fell on to the grass with a sickening thud. It was a long, nightmare moment before she managed to extricate herself from beneath him, but at last she struggled free and with her remaining strength pulled him clear of the flames and rolled him to safety down the incline.

By now the car was a burning mass of fire, and making sure that Matthew was out of reach of any sparks, she limped slowly up the bank to the road. It was deserted and she sank down on the side and began to cry.

She was aroused by a squeal of brakes and Ted's voice, urgent with fear. "What's happened, Mrs. Armstrong? Where's Matt?"

"They hit him," she gasped. "The car ran off the road and caught fire. He's the other side of the bank."

"Take it easy, lass. It's all right now. Jess, look after Stella, I think she's going to faint. I'll signal another car to fetch an ambulance. If Matt's unconscious we'd best not move him in case he's badly hurt."

Within twenty minutes Matthew was being driven to Leeds Infirmary and Stella was lying in the back of Ted's car.

"We'd best get you home," he said.

"I want to go to the hospital."

"You can't help Matt any more," Jess interrupted. "He'll be well looked after. But if you're not in bed soon we'll have another casualty on our hands."

Stella remembered little of her arrival at Grey Walls. The doctor came to bandage her swollen ankle and give her a sedative, but she was too overwhelmed for it to take full effect, and she passed the night in fitful sleep.

It was still barely light when Jess appeared at the door in her dressing-gown. "I wondered whether you were awake," she said gruffly. "You might like to know I 'phoned the hospital. Matt was unconscious all night but the X-rays show nothing and they think it's concussion. Anyway they said he'd be fine in a few days."

Tears poured down Stella's cheeks and she turned her face into the pillows. "When he slumped over the wheel I thought they'd killed him. It was horrible — I was so frightened, and then the fire . . . I didn't think I'd get him out in time!"

"Well you did, so don't fret." Jess bent over her. "You were fine, Stella — Matt owes his life to you.

Now go back to sleep. It's still early and I'll bring you a cup of tea later on."

It was two days before the doctor allowed Stella to get up, and she spent the time deciding what to do. The position between herself and Matthew was unchanged: if anything it was worse, for he would feel more under an obligation to her than ever. For his sake she must go, even if the thought of not seeing him again filled her with a sadness as inexplicable as it was unexpected.

When Jess came to see her on the third morning she was already dressed, her suitcases locked and by the door.

"So you're going after all?" Jess said. "I wondered if you would change your mind."

"What's happened hasn't altered the situation."

"Wouldn't you rather wait and talk to Matthew first?"

Stella did not look up from collecting her trinkets on the dressing-table. "I thought you would be glad I'm going. It's what you've always wanted."

"I'll not deny that. But if it would make any difference to you and Matt I'd be willing to move out. I've a fancy to live in Cleethorpes near my friends."

"It's too late to make any difference now," Stella replied steadily. "Matthew will be happier when I have gone."

Jess shrugged. "I daresay you'll be happier too, with someone of your own sort. Will you see Matt before you leave?"

"No."

"Any message for him?"

"Just that I hope he gets better quickly."

"Right, I'll tell him." Jess extended her hand. "It's a pity things have turned out the way they have, but thanks for saving Matt's life. He'd probably like to thank you himself . . . Are you sure you won't change your mind?"

"Positive, thanks."

As soon as all her belongings were packed, Stella went downstairs. There was only Elsie to say good-bye to her, waving as the cab moved down the drive. The house seemed warmer and far more friendly when she turned to look back, the bright flowers round the lawns giving it a richness lacking during winter. But she had left no mark upon it, and in a few short hours it would be as if she had never lived there at all.

She managed to find a corner seat in the train and sat looking out with unseeing eyes as the engine gathered speed and the clackety-clack of the wheels sang a song of no return. This journey was different from all others, an end instead of a beginning, and remembering her lack of understanding with Matthew, she turned away to hide her tears. Of course he had had to return to fight the strike — he was a born fighter and she, his wife, who should have done everything in her power to help him, had been the only one to defeat him. Small wonder he wanted her to go!

She had wired her mother the time of her arrival, but when she reached King's Cross there was no familiar face to greet her and she took a cab straight to Knightsbridge. The front door of the flat was as shabby as ever, and she put her key into the lock with a dull sense of finality. She was home, but with no sense of belonging any more, and she looked around with the critical eye of a stranger, bracing herself as she walked across the hall to the drawing-room.

Her mother was sitting playing Patience. "My dear, how lovely to see you!"

Stella ran across and embraced her so convulsively that Mrs. Percy drew back in surprise. "Why, darling, what's the matter?"

"Everything, Mother!" She burst into tears. "I've left Matthew — for good!"

CHAPTER TWELVE

MATTHEW was lying propped up by pillows on the narrow white hospital bed when Jess opened the door and came in.

"It's good to see you looking more like yourself." She kissed his cheek. "How do you feel?"

"Not bad." He touched the bandage on his head. "This makes me look worse than I am."

"It was quite a crack, so you'd better not be in a hurry to get up. I've brought you some fruit and books."

"Thanks." His eyes searched her face. "I was hoping Stella would come with you. How is she?"

"Fine. She hopes you'll get better soon."

He turned his head on the pillow. "Ted was here before you and he said she saved my life. Tell her to come and see me. I want to thank her."

"You'll have to write," Jess said bluntly. "She's gone."

He was suddenly very still, his skin grey. "Gone where?"

"To London. Perhaps I shouldn't have told you so soon, but I didn't think it would be a surprise. After all, you knew she was going."

"When I heard how wonderful she had been, I thought . . . I hoped . . ." he sighed. "More fool me."

"I know what you hoped," Jess said awkwardly, "but Stella helped you the same way she would have helped anyone."

"You mean she only did for me what she'd have done for a stranger?" He closed his eyes. "I suppose you're right. It seems I'll never learn — not even the hard way."

"I'm sorry it's turned out like this."

164

"Are you? I expected you to say 'I told you so.' You've every right to — you warned me in the beginning."

"I know, but that was before I understood how much she meant to you."

"And still does."

"Then why did you act so stupidly?" Jess burst out. "It was crazy of you to go to Belle because you quarrelled with Stella. You may be clever in business but you know nothing about women! No girl would stay with her husband if she knew he'd gone to another woman just because they had a row!"

"Stella didn't love me when she married me," Matthew said quietly.

"I guessed that."

He hesitated. "We were never man and wife either."

Jess caught her breath. "So that was it! Well, even if she had wanted to change her mind about you, pride wouldn't have let her after you went to Belle. She was wrong to give you a reason to go, but you were wrong to take it! Not many women would have forgiven you — you have to love a man very much for that. It's when you don't love him that you expect such a lot from him."

A grim smile lifted the corners of his mouth. "Then she must have loved me very little indeed."

The silence lengthened and Jess stood up. "The best thing to do is cut your losses and begin again."

"I don't intend to marry anyone else, if that's what you mean!" A feverish patch of colour stained his cheeks. "I'm not a young man to let myself in for something like this a second time."

"You're not old either! How do you intend to spend the rest of your life — with Belle?"

He shook his head. "I've lost my taste for just any woman. It's either the right one or none at all."

"Well, the sooner you're better the sooner you'll

have something to occupy your mind. You'd best concentrate on getting fit."

In the ensuing days Matthew could think of nothing except Stella, her face constantly in his mind's eye as he brooded over the past unhappy months. What high hopes he had cherished when he had brought her to Grey Walls, and how quickly misunderstandings had put an end to them! Would it have been different if they had gone away on their honeymoon or would she have turned against him in any case? Was Jess right when she had said that by going to Belle he had made it impossible for Stella to stay even if she had wanted to? Whatever way he looked at it, he and Stella had been incompatible from the beginning: only his blind folly had stopped him realizing it.

Yet he could not stop himself from reliving the hours when he had held her in his arms, when — after her first terror — she had clung to him and returned his kisses, wanting him as much as he had wanted her. But it was crazy to interpret that as love; all it proved was his expertise as a lover and Stella's ability to respond to it. He had to stop thinking about her. Had to make his life again.

So persistently did he argue with his doctor, that within ten days of the accident he was back at his desk, working with such intensity that his staff began to dread his arrival in the morning.

Not even his most intimate friends knew Stella had left him, and if they wondered at her absence, they respected his privacy too well to question him. The only person who ventured to ask him about it was Ned, who did so when the two men sat alone over coffee and brandy after dinner one evening.

"There are a few rumours floating around about you and Stella," he said casually. "Don't you think you ought to do something about it? People are talking."

"Let 'em talk! Keep their tongues wagging about

one thing and they'll not wag about something else."

Ned's face creased into an awkward grin. "Well, you've given 'em enough gossip in the past few months to last a lifetime. I suppose it's none of my business, but if it would help you to talk about it . . ."

Matthew rubbed his hand over his eyes. "I'll tell you one day, Ned — I'd rather not talk about it now."

Although at one time Matthew would have ridiculed the suggestion that a woman's presence could remain long after she had gone, wherever he went in Grey Walls he was reminded of Stella. It was hard to believe a person of such nebulous qualities should have imprinted her personality so deeply, but a bowl of flowers set on the dark table of the hall, the open lid of the piano or even the firelight shadowing the room — brought her so vividly to mind that he could not bear to be at home for long, and when he was not working at the office he would tramp the countryside for miles, returning so exhausted that he would fall asleep the instant he flung himself on the bed.

For Stella, too, the time dragged. It was impossible to lead the life she had lived before her marriage. Meeting married girl friends brought home to her the ambiguity of her own position, and as the weeks passed she dropped out of circulation. It was hard, too, to bear her mother's assumption that she had left Matthew because of Charles, and though at first she had been too weary to argue with her, once the emotional upheaval of her return home wore off, her natural resilience came back.

"I knew your marriage wouldn't be a success," Mrs. Percy said complacently, one morning a month after her return. "I had a feeling Fate was planning something for Charles, but when it did, you were already tied to that boor."

"Don't call Matthew a boor! And I've already told you my leaving him had nothing to do with Charles."

"You might not think so consciously, but I'm sure it was in the back of your mind. You know you only need say the word and he'll ask you to marry him."

"As I'm still married to Matthew, that would be difficult."

"Really Stella. Yorkshire not only sharpened your appetite, it's sharpened your temper too."

"Sorry Mother, but it's your own fault. Don't keep going on about my marrying Charles."

"But he's so right for you."

"I'm not free," Stella hedged.

"You can soon change that. Matthew surely won't try to keep you? He always struck me as the sort of man who'd cut his losses as fast as he could."

"You're probably right," Stella said. "But I intend leaving it to *him*. At the moment I'm concerned with getting a job."

"What nonsense! Matthew must support you."

"There's no must about it! You can't say anything nice about him, yet you'd be quite happy to see him keeping me!"

"One thing has nothing to do with the other. Some husbands are monsters, but they still keep their wives in luxury."

"Matthew isn't a monster and I don't want to be kept in luxury! I've accepted quite enough from him already, without taking any more."

"Rubbish! It's only right —"

"Hullo, you two! Am I interrupting a row?"

They looked round as Adrian came into the room, preposterously good-looking in blue sweater and slacks.

"Have you had tea?" his mother asked.

"No, Ma, I'd love some. I won't be having supper till late — going to the theatre."

"Then I'll make you some sandwiches as well."

Mrs. Percy hurried out and Stella wondered why

168

mothers spoilt their sons so much more than their daughters.

Adrian sprawled in an armchair. "You're looking serious, old girl."

"I was thinking what a lot of good it would do you to go away from home and stand on your own feet."

"What would I use for money? Matthew's allowance barely covers my expenses living at home. It certainly wouldn't stretch to digs."

"You may soon have to manage without his allowance altogether."

He was immediately on the alert. "Are you joking?"

"No, I've left Matthew and I'd rather you didn't go on accepting money from him."

"Changed your tune all of a sudden, haven't you?" he said. "One of your reasons for marrying him was to help me."

"Only *one* of the reasons," she echoed. "I also thought we stood a chance of being happy together — that our marriage would work out. Unfortunately it didn't, and it would make things less embarrassing if we didn't accept any more help from him."

"Forget the 'we'," Adrian said. *"You* needn't accept anything if you don't want to, but it doesn't embarrass *me* to do so."

"Well it should! I don't want you to take any more money from him."

"No can do," he said laconically, and suddenly lost his temper. "Darn it all, Stella, you can't expect me to leave the Academy now. I'm just beginning to get somewhere . . . to attract attention. I won't give it up — and certainly not in order to save your pride! You should have thought of that before you started the whole thing. You've no right to back down now."

"Things have changed."

"For you, maybe. Not for me. The piano is the only thing I care about."

"And gambling!"

"Yes, you can fling that at me. But I haven't asked you for anything lately, have I?"

"I should hope not!"

"I won't either." He was serious. "That part of my life is finished. From now on it's music. Believe me, Stella, I mean it."

Her anger evaporated as she looked into his eyes. "*I'll* try and pay for your tuition. I'll get a job and give you every penny."

He whistled soundlessly. "You really do care about taking Matthew's money. I hadn't realised . . ." He shrugged. "But the whole discussion is academic. He's already paid the fees for the whole time I'm likely to be there, and fixed an allowance for me too."

"*What?* But when?"

"I got a letter from a firm of stockbrokers this morning. They said he had invested some money with them and arranged for me to have the interest on it for the next five years. I guess he must have known what you wanted to do. This is his way of showing you it isn't necessary."

Speechless, Stella buried her head in her hands. She was conscious of Adrian coming to stand beside her, and felt his hand stroking her hair.

"Don't be upset, Stell. If Matthew hadn't wanted to help me — if he thought we were taking advantage of him — he would have stopped my allowance like a shot. I don't know why you left him — at least not the real reason — but whatever it is, he still *wants* to help you. Making this arrangement for me, is his way of letting you know it."

"I suppose so," she sighed. "But it puts me so much in his debt."

"Perhaps he feels in *your* debt too."

Mrs. Percy's entrance with the trolley prevented further conversation, and Stella went to her room, anxious to be alone. Talking about Matthew brought him so vividly to mind that she could almost imagine he was here. Going to the window, she pushed it wide open, longing for a breath of the pure, fresh air that blew in from the moors and the sound of a blunt Yorkshire voice. How warm and real Matthew was compared with the husbands of her friends; how much more down to earth and natural! Resting her cheek against the curtain she tried to hold back her tears. "What have I thrown away?" she cried. "What can I do with the rest of my life?"

The door opened and Mrs. Percy came in with a cup of tea. "Do have this, darling. It will do you good." She studied her daughter carefully. "Adrian just told me what Matthew has done. It was rather — rather nice of him."

"Yes," Stella said automatically.

"You shouldn't let it worry you. He can easily afford it." Then hastily: "I mean think how pleased he'll be when Adrian's a success. He'll be able to say *he* helped him achieve it!"

This was the last credit in the world Stella could envisage Matthew claiming. How little her mother understood his genuine kindness. "Adrian has to *be* a success first," she commented dryly.

"He will."

"How can you be so sure?"

"Because I know him." Seeing her daughter's sarcastic look, she said defensively: "Wait till you have a son of your own. Then you'll understand."

Stella set down her cup. She had never thought about children. Now the idea of a sturdy little boy with Matthew's blunt features and bright blue eyes tugged at her imagination.

"Stella, I'm talking to you."

"Sorry, I didn't hear."

171

"I was saying Charles is coming to see you this evening."

"Charles? How does he know I'm home?"

"My dear girl, you didn't want me to keep it a secret, did you? He rang to see how I was, and naturally I told him you'd left Matthew."

"You shouldn't have done that."

"Why not? He has to know some time. Really Stella, you can't go on living like a hermit."

"Possibly not. But I don't think it's wise to start up with Charles again."

"You'll change your mind when you see him."

Watching Charles as he entered the room later that evening, Stella could understand her mother's attitude. How perfectly he epitomized Prince Charming! Good-looking in a not too masculine and aggressive way; charming of manner and gentle of speaking, he was every young girl's dream of the ideal husband.

Remembering the last time they had met, and what had happened to her afterwards, her greeting of him was somewhat stilted, but his pleasure at seeing her again took the edge off her unease, and soon she was talking to him without embarrassment. It was only when her mother left them alone, ostensibly to watch a television programme, that her awkwardness returned.

"Don't look so worried," Charles said easily. "You needn't tell me why you left Matthew if you don't want to."

"There's nothing to tell." He looked so disbelieving that she was forced to continue. "We both realised our marriage was a mistake. Neither of us was happy and it — it seemed better to part."

"You made the right decision. I'm glad. Very glad."

She moistened her lips. He expected her to say more yet she could not say what he wanted to hear. "I haven't changed my mind about us. What I said

to you the last time we met . . . that I don't love
you . . . I still mean it. I like you Charles — more
than anyone else I know — but I don't love you."

If he was disappointed he did not show it. "How
can you be so sure? You're still upset at leaving
Armstrong. Even though you didn't love him, ending
a marriage isn't easy. I suggest we don't talk about
the future yet."

Restlessly she rose and paced the room. "You're
wrong, Charles. I mean about my being too upset
to know my own mind. I know it very well. And I
won't change it either." Determinedly she faced him.
"I don't love you and I don't want to marry you. It
would be wrong of me to let you believe otherwise."

Carefully he crossed one leg over the other. "If I
didn't know you better, I'd say you were in love
with Armstrong."

"Would it be so incredible if I were?"

Charles let out his breath in a sigh. "Then why
on earth did you leave him?"

"Because you can't build a marriage on a rotten
foundation; and there are certain things neither of us
can forget."

"So you're going to forget each other instead!"

"Yes."

"And if you can't? Will you go back to him?"

"He wouldn't have me."

"I see." Charles came over and put his hand beneath her chin, tilting it so that he could look into
her face. "Are you sure you haven't built Armstrong
up into some romantic, hard-done-by figure? I don't
know what happened between you after I left that
night, but whatever it was, don't let yourself be con-
fused by it. Armstrong knew how you felt about him
when he married you. If he got the raw end of the
deal, he only has himself to blame. You pity him —
nothing more than that."

"You're very sure of what you say."

"I have to be," he said dryly. "It's my only hope." He released her and went to the door. "I'll leave you alone for a few months. If you want to see me before then, you know where to contact me."

"Thank you, Charles. You're very understanding."

"It may well be my epitaph," he said and walked out.

With a cry Stella sank down on the settee. Was Charles right in believing she was confusing pity with love? Could her feeling for Matthew merely be a desire to make amends for the shabby way she had treated him? If this were so, surely his going to Belle would have expurged her guilt? Yet despite knowing that he had turned to another woman, she still longed to comfort him, still wanted to remove the hurt from his eyes and the beaten curve from his shoulders. Yes, what she felt for Matthew *was* pity, but that did not mean it wasn't love! Indeed every woman who loved a man knew there was an element of compassion in all love worthy of the name; knew that beneath a man's strength was the deep need for the comfort of a woman's arms.

With all her heart she longed to give Matthew the tenderness she had never shown him before. If only she had allowed her first instinct about him to take its natural course! Had not been too bigoted to see beneath the manners to the man. But like a child she had looked in vain for a real-life version of the hero she had dreamed about, allowing a figment of her imagination to obscure the real worth of the man she had married.

CHAPTER THIRTEEN

STELLA'S decision to get a job was easier said than done, for without training or business experience she was offered such ill-paid posts that it would not have been worth her while to accept any of them.

It was, ironically, through Adrian that she at last managed to find a suitable position. The father of one of the boys at the Academy was a Harley Street doctor who had recently lost his receptionist, and Adrian casually suggested she went to see him.

With some misgivings she did so, and found Dr. Carlisle a charming, grey-haired man who engaged her on the spot.

"I don't think your lack of experience matters at all," he said. "What I need is someone with a pleasant manner, who can book appointments and receive my patients. There's very little typing to be done, though the hours are somewhat long."

"I don't mind what hours I put in, Dr. Carlisle."

"Then we should get on extremely well!"

Within minutes salary and duties had been amicably settled, and Stella returned home feeling happier than she had for a long time.

Working for a living gave her no chance to brood, and only during the weekends — when she went for long, solitary walks in Hyde Park — was Matthew constantly in her mind. Every man she had met in recent months seemed pallid by comparison, and she would have given a great deal to hear her husband's gruff voice and see his strong, masculine face with its firm mouth and blunt, determined chin.

Yet she could not live forever in this limbo; sooner or later she must make a fuller life for herself, and even though the thought of marrying again seemed impossible, she was too much of a realist not to accept the fact that one day she would do so. But could her future be with Charles? As always, she found it disquieting to try and imagine a specific man taking Matthew's place; a second marriage was acceptable only as long as she could think of it in abstract terms; to consider it in emotional ones only made her realise how deep her feelings for Matthew were.

In an effort to stop thinking about the past she had her hair cut short. Matthew had liked it long, and to cut it seemed the first step in her emancipation from him. But unfortunately it worked in reverse, for the new style — her soft blonde hair curling softly on her forehead and around her ears — made her look so much younger and appealing that she knew he would have liked it even more. If only she could see him again — meet him accidentally and catch him off guard — who knew what might happen? But this was so unlikely that she forced herself not to think about it, and instead concentrated even harder on her work.

"You haven't had a date for months," her mother remarked one Sunday afternoon in late summer. "Why don't you ring up some of your girlfriends? They must be tired of getting in touch with you."

"They probably are. But I can't bear it when they try and pretend how lucky I am not to be tied down by a husband and children. I feel they're sorry for me."

"You could soon put an end to that. Charles would —"

"Not Charles, Mother. Don't start that again!"

"I'm only thinking of *you*. I can't bear to see you so unhappy. You've got to do something with your life, Stella. You can't go on like this. Why don't you see a lawyer about a divorce?"

It was a question Stella had recently asked herself. Now, with her mother posing it, she was forced to find an answer. "I was waiting to see what Matthew was going to do . . . what he wanted."

"What *he* wanted?" her mother said furiously. "Why should you care what *he* wants? It's what you want that matters."

Stella turned away. If only it were as easy as that. What she wanted. Matthew . . . Matthew. I want *him*, she thought.

"Stella!" Mrs. Percy gasped. "You can't mean it!"

Stella swung round, and only as she saw her mother's horrified face did she realise she had spoken her thoughts aloud.

"Yes," she said quietly. "I do mean it. I've been in love with him for a long while, but I was too stupid — too prejudiced to realise it."

"It's impossible. He's such a —"

"Mother!" Stella said angrily. "Whatever you say won't change facts. I love him. If you hadn't made your dislike of him so obvious I —"

"So now you're putting the blame on me! I might have known."

"I don't blame you at all. I blame myself. I should never have let myself be swayed by *your* standards."

"What's wrong with my standards?"

"They died with Queen Victoria!"

"They used to be good enough for you!"

"That shows what a fool I was."

"And now you've come to your senses I suppose?"

"Yes. But too late. Matthew wouldn't have me even if I went back to him."

"He wouldn't have *you?*" Mrs. Percy looked incredulous. "You must be joking. I should have thought he'd be only too pleased to have you back."

About to reply, Stella stopped: some things were too intimate to be discussed. "Let's change the subject, Mother. It's a waste of time to go on with this."

"Very well." Mrs. Percy went to the door. "Neither of us will change and it's pointless arguing who's

177

right or wrong. All I want is your happiness, and if that means you returning to —"

"I can't go back. I've already told you!"

"You can't seem to go forward either! Think that one over before you get too old!"

Sitting alone by the window, Stella absorbed the remark, realising its validity with a depression so deep that it was like a physical pain. Her mother was right, of course. One day — and not too far in the future either — she must come to terms with herself. Either forget pride and beg Matthew to take her back, or marry another man and force herself to forget him. Which would be the harder to do?

Restlessly she wandered round the room, fiddling with the ornaments, straightening cushions and glancing idly at some magazines on a side table before she finally sat down at the piano. Her hands drifted over the keys and a gentle Chopin *Etude* floated into the air. As always, music soothed her, and when she came to the end she remained where she was, her expression brooding and sad. Then her fingers moved again, but this time it was the Yorkshire melody she had played to taunt Matthew the night Charles had first dined with them. How different the sound was now: tender and gay, romantic and gentle, no longer the vulgar sound she had so cruelly strummed all those months ago. Matthew, she cried silently. Matthew . . .

The insistent pealing of the doorbell brought her back to the present, and with an exclamation she hurried to answer it. Bother Adrian for forgetting his keys. It was the third time this week.

"All right," she said crossly, "I'm coming."

She flung open the door and stopped, staring at the young woman in a yellow linen suit who stood on the threshold. "I'm sorry," Stella said. "I thought it was my brother. Can I help you?"

The girl nodded, her thick black hair swinging

178

either side of a vividly made-up face. "I'd like to talk to you."

Her voice was as soft and full as her figure, with a North country twang that made Stella's heart miss a beat. "I'm afraid I don't know you," she said uncertainly.

"I'm Belle."

Without a word Stella went to close the door, but the girl put her foot in the way and pushed forward.

"I intend speaking to you, Mrs. Armstrong, so you may as well let me in. Otherwise I'll talk to you from here!"

Rigidly Stella led the way into the drawing-room. "Well," she said, standing tense and nervous in the centre of the room. "Say what you have to and leave!"

Unperturbed, Belle sat down and crossed her legs. "I've come to talk about Matt."

"So I imagined. But I would rather you didn't."

"You're labouring under a delusion, Mrs. Armstrong," the girl continued, ignoring the comment, "and I've come to put you right. But I'd like to know one thing first — do you love Matt?"

"That's none of your business!"

Belle smiled. "If you didn't, you would have said so — so it looks as though you do!" Bracelets jangled as she leaned forward. "He's eating his heart out for you. For heaven's sake go back before it's too late."

"It's too late already."

"You're wrong. That's what I've come to tell you. I knew Matt before he married you — there's no secret about that — but I never expected to see him *after* he was married."

Stella jumped up. "I don't want to hear!"

"You must! When he came to my flat in the middle of the night he was out of his mind with grief. I knew —"

"Be quiet!" Stella cried.

"I won't! You've got to hear me. When he kissed me I knew something terrible had happened to him. He was like a wounded animal running to the only hide-out he knew. He hadn't come to me because he wanted me, but because he'd nowhere else to go!" She leaned closer still. "When he came back the following night I —"

"Don't go on," Stella begged, her voice broken. "I can't bear it."

"You've got to hear the truth. It's important. After that first night — when he cried in my arms like a baby — he never made love to me again. Never!"

Stella began to tremble. "What are you — what are you trying to say?"

"That Matt wasn't having an affair with me. After that one night he never touched me."

"Never . . ." Stella moistened her lips. "Why did he pretend?"

"Surely you know the answer to that?" Belle said dryly. "Pride. He thought you loved someone else, so he saved face by pretending he didn't care. Being seen with me was the obvious solution."

Stella sat down again, trying to absorb what she had just learned. But it was not easy: so much of what she believed had to be discarded. "Does Matthew know you've come to see me?" she asked at last.

"Not likely! He'd have my scalp if he knew! I've only seen him once since he left hospital. He came to tell me he wouldn't be seeing me anymore. He didn't say why — he's too kind for that — but he didn't need to. It was obvious. Once you'd gone, there was no need for him to pretend." She sighed and lifted her shoulders. "There was no need for him to stop seeing me either. With you out of the way, he was free to do as he liked. But he'd changed. A blind man can see that!" She regarded Stella with unabashed curiosity. "Why did you leave without putting up a fight for him?"

Stella hesitated, unwilling to be rude, yet equally unwilling to lie. "I . . . I'm afraid I . . ." She swallowed. "I don't believe in the permissive society."

It took a moment for the statement to register. "You mean because he came to me?"

"Yes. I — I couldn't forgive him."

"There was nothing to forgive." The full voice was laconic. "That night — even when he came to me — it was hopeless. It was either you or no-one."

Stella could not hide her joy, and seeing it, Belle flushed angrily. "You're not against the permissive society, Mrs. Armstrong, you're against forgiveness and understanding! Against pity and compassion! Maybe I shouldn't speak to you like this but —"

"No! You're right. Everything you've said is true." Pacing the floor, Stella no longer monitored her words. "I was so concerned about my own feelings that I didn't think about anyone else's. Matthew hurt me and I couldn't forgive him. But it wasn't only because of you. There was more to it than that."

"Jess, I suppose?"

"Jess, and his attitude to work and my being alone so much . . . It seems stupid and pointless now, but at the time . . ."

"If you had loved him it wouldn't have mattered."

"If *he* loved *me*, it wouldn't have happened!"

Belle nodded. "You've a point there. That's one thing I can't figure out — why he let you go without putting up a fight. Matt's not a quitter, yet with you . . . he just gave in."

Stella did not answer; even the intimacy of this moment could not make her disclose Matthew's reasons, and she watched in silence as Belle picked up her handbag and went to the door.

"I've said what I came for, Mrs. Armstrong. The rest is up to you."

Impulsively Stella held out her hand. "Thank you

for coming to see me. I don't know why you did, but —"

"For Matt," came the retort. "He deserves the best, but he obviously wants you!"

Stella drew a sharp breath. "You don't mince words."

"If I did, I wouldn't have come here."

The door closed behind her and Stella stared at it blindly, lost in thought. A noise from the kitchen made her remember her mother was home, and unwilling to talk to anyone she hurried into her bedroom and locked the door.

Only in the safety of her room did the barriers she had been maintaining since Belle's arrival, dissolve, and she sank on the bed and cried: for the wasted months, the unnecessary suffering which she and Matthew had caused each other. It was easy to understand why he had wanted to save his pride, especially in the beginning when she had rejected him so cruelly, but surely after his accident he had realised how she felt about him? Or had the hurt she had inflicted gone so deep that it could not be forgotten?

Feverishly she jumped up and began to pack. She had to see him; had to tell him that she loved him. He might not believe her, might even send her away again — despite what Belle had said about his loving her — but no matter what he did, she had to tell him the truth.

"Stella," her mother called. "Where are you?"

"In here." Stella opened the door and her mother came into the room, stopping abruptly at the sight of the cases on the floor.

"You're going back."

It was statement, not a question, and Stella nodded. "I should never have left."

"Are you *sure* it's what you want?"

"It's the only thing I *am* sure about."

Mrs. Percy sighed. "I hope things work out for you. If they don't, you always have a home here."

Tears flowed down Stella's cheeks and wordlessly she put her arms around her mother's shoulders mentally closer to her than they had been for a long time.

CHAPTER FOURTEEN

STELLA reached Grey Walls in the middle of the following afternoon, and watched with thumping heart as the driver carried her cases to the front door. He drove off before she rang the bell and she waited apprehensively as footsteps crossed the hall and Jess opened the door.

"So you've come back!" Jess stepped aside to let her in and Stella lifted her suitcases into the hall. "Matt never mentioned you were coming."

"He doesn't know. How — how is he?"

"Well enough in the circumstances."

"What time will he be home?"

"He didn't say he'd be late, though since you've gone he spends more time at the factory than here! Been none too easy to live with, either — bites my head off for the least word. I was going to be in this evening, but as you're back, I'll spend the night at Milly's."

"There's no need for you to go," Stella said hastily.

Jess shrugged. "I'll have to be going anyway, so I might as well get used to it. I'll not live here now you're back. It didn't work last time and it won't work now."

"Perhaps this time we'll have a better understanding."

"Enough understanding to know we won't get on." She moved towards the kitchen. "I'll give Elsie instructions for the meal. After tomorrow you can take over completely."

She went out and Stella heaved a sigh of relief. At least one of the obstacles to her and Matthew's happiness had been removed; the rest was up to her.

Almost before she was aware of it, it was time to

184

get ready for dinner, and she changed into the chartreuse green dress Matthew liked, wondering as she did so what he would think of her hair. He had always liked it long and free, and on the infrequent occasions when she had let him kiss her, had run his fingers lovingly through the soft mass. She longed for him to do it again and with a twinge of fear wondered what would become of her if he refused to take her back.

Afraid of being alone with her thoughts she went downstairs, but Jess had already left the house and she occupied herself by setting the dining-room table with lace mats and filling a shallow bowl with roses as a centrepiece, putting two candles on the table before she filled another vase and placed it in the hall.

It was growing dark when she had finished and a faint breeze was blowing in from the moors. She went to the window and stood looking out over the garden. It was the first time she had seen it in high summer and in the deepening twilight it had a soft magic, a scent of night stocks drifting in from the flower-beds. Even the house seemed softer, the grey stone warm and homely, and with a sigh she lit the candles before going into the drawing-room to listen for Matthew.

She did not have long to wait. Within a few minutes a car crunched on the gravel, a man's heavy tread mounted the steps and there was the sound of a key in the lock.

Quivering with nervousness she got to her feet. Matthew's steps crossed to the dining-room and stopped short, and she guessed he had seen the candlelight. There was silence before he came back across the hall, then the drawing-room door opened and he came in.

Neither of them spoke as he closed the door and leaned against it. Stella thought how much older he looked, how thin and lined, his hair more noticeably grey, his shoulders stooping.

Her hands went out to him. "Matthew, I — I've come home."

"What for?" he asked grimly.

"Because I've been a fool. Oh, Matthew, I'm sorry!"

"I don't want your pity."

"I'm not offering you pity. I'm offering you love! Oh Matthew, why didn't you tell me about Belle? She came to see me and told me everything." He did not answer and she struggled with tears. "I've been cruel and blind, but you never even gave me the opportunity to understand. Why didn't you come after me and give us a chance to start again? Didn't you realize when I saved your life that I loved you?"

"Why should I have realized?" he asked bitterly. "You only did for me what you'd have done for anyone else! I'd fooled myself enough about you without fooling myself any more! I had plenty of time to think when I was in hospital, and it didn't make pretty thinking either. I was a fool from the word go where you were concerned. When I came down to London the first time and found you with Charles I should have realized what you thought of me. But I was so mad about you, it didn't seem to matter. I've taken more from you than I'd ever take from anyone else, man or woman, and I'll never do it again." He passed a hand over his eyes. "That's why I didn't come after you. From now on I stay where I am and as I am."

Tears streamed down her cheeks and she swallowed convulsively.

"Why are you crying?" he demanded harshly. "Isn't our reunion going as you planned?"

"I didn't plan it!" she cried. "I came back because I wanted to, not because I'd thought it all out beforehand."

"What would have happened if Belle hadn't come to see you?" he asked sardonically. "Would you have gone on languishing in London, or was your vanity pleased to find no other woman meant anything to me?"

"I didn't come back because of that, but because Belle said you — you still loved me." Stella dashed the tears from her cheeks. "I know you think I'm hard and cold, but I wasn't vain enough to think I still meant anything to you. After the way I'd behaved I thought you hated me."

"And when you found I didn't — that I couldn't bear to touch another woman — you decided to come back and forgive me!" He gave a harsh laugh. "Well, I can do without that sort of forgiveness!"

"I'm not forgiving *you*," she cried. "I want you to forgive *me*."

"Me?"

"Yes. Forgive me for the way I treated you . . . for being so bigoted that I couldn't admit I loved you. If you won't let me live with you again, at least try to stop hating me."

"I don't hate you," he said quietly. "I could never do that."

She waited, hoping against hope he would continue, but he said no more and, not trusting herself to look at him, she spoke again. "I'd be lying if I said that learning about Belle — knowing you hadn't . . . Of course it made a difference to me! But I'd have come back in any case. It might not have been today or even next week, but I'd have come back eventually."

"Eventually," he echoed with heavy sarcasm. "When would that have been?"

"When I had proved to myself that I could stand on my own feet. When I could show you I wasn't coming back because I needed your help." Still he said nothing and she stumbled to the door. "I shouldn't have come. Seeing me again has reminded you of things you'd rather forget. I'm sorry, Matthew."

"Wait a moment, Stella." His voice was a whisper. "There's something I'd like to know. People don't

187

change because you want them to — that would be
Utopia! And that's what I can't understand about
you. Why should you love me now when you only
despised me before?"

"I never despised you!" She spoke to the door,
unable to look at him. "On our wedding night I was
afraid of you — that's why I was so cruel — and
the night I found out about Belle . . ." She clenched
her hands. "I was so hurt I just wanted to hurt you
back."

"You're forgetting one more night," he reminded
her.

"I can never forget that," she whispered. "It made
me realise I could never belong to anyone except
you." Nerving herself she turned and looked at him.
"I didn't say anything cruel to you that night, Matthew, and I didn't go on fighting you either! From the
moment you kissed me — held me — I tried to let
you know I loved you." She lowered her head, her
words almost inaudible. "I obviously didn't succeed."

"Stella!" In two strides he was beside her, gripping
her shoulders so violently that she winced. "Of course
I knew! But I was afraid to believe it. I wanted you
so much that I thought I'd imagined your response."
One hand cupped her face, forcing her to look at
him. "Why me?" he asked fiercely. "Why me when
you can have Charles? He's your sort of person, Stella.
He can give you everything you want."

"I want you!" she cried.

Still he hesitated. "There'll be no going back. If
you stay now, I'll never let you go."

"I won't want to. My place is with you. Hold me,
Matthew. Hold me and say you love me!"

For a long moment he looked into her eyes, then
fumblingly drew her against him and rested his cheek
against hers. "Don't you know you're my whole life
without me having to tell you?" His voice was low
and broken. "It was no good when you were gone.

The factory, my home, my friends — they all meant nothing if you weren't here to share them."

"I'll always be here. You'll never be alone again."

A shudder went through him and he held her so closely that she could feel the heavy pounding of his heart. "I still can't believe it . . . to have you say you love me . . . It's like a dream." He stroked her hair and then held her slightly away. "You've cut it."

Her eyes crinkled. "I'll grow it again if you want."

For answer he bent his head and pressed his lips to the lobe of her ear. "No," he said thickly, "keep it short. I can see more of you to kiss!"

Twining her arms around his neck she pressed her body against his. "We've a lot of time to make up for, Matthew."

"Don't remind me." He went to kiss her mouth and then stopped, his expression so dark that she was afraid.

"What's wrong, Matthew? You look angry."

"Only with myself. I wasn't blameless. I realise that. But this time we'll start our marriage properly. Jess will have to find a place of her own."

"She's already told me she will."

"Ah." It was a satisfied sound. "That's the main problem out of the way. The next thing is our honeymoon. Does Venice appeal to you?"

"I don't need a honeymoon. I'm happy as long as we're together."

"No," he said firmly. "I want you completely to myself. Or does the thought scare you?"

Stella put her hands behind his head and pulled it down until her mouth found his. "Does this answer your question?" she asked against his lips.

"It's a good beginning," he replied. "But I'd like a longer answer!"

Blushing, she started to give it to him.

HARLEQUIN OMNIBUS

☐ **VIOLET WINSPEAR**

Palace Of The Peacocks (#1318)

Beloved Tyrant (#1032)

Court Of The Veils (#1267)

$1.50

☐ **ISOBEL CHACE**

A Handful Of Silver (#1306)

The Saffron Sky (#1250)

The Damask Rose (#1334)

$1.50

☐ **JOYCE DINGWELL**

The Feel Of Silk (#1342)

A Taste For Love (#1229)

Will You Surrender (#1179)

$1.50

☐ **SUSAN BARRIE**

Marry A Stranger (#1043)

The Marriage Wheel (#1311)

Rose In The Bud (#1168)

$1.50

THE 3 IN 1 VOLUME — EACH VOLUME
BY THE SAME AUTHOR — ONLY $1.50 EACH.